PLOTTING MURDER:

A Creative Guide to Countless, Detailed Plotlines

J.J. Counsilman

22 mind maps, 100 story premises, 50 plot twists, 50 story endings, and 3 stories from plotlines

[Second Edition]

Other books by J.J. Counsilman:

Journey Into A Far Country: A Novel of Love and Prejudice in Modern China. SinoAmerican Books (Second Edition, 2015).

Becoming Tough. SinoAmerican Books (Third Edition, 2007).

The Superior Men Of Xinjiang. SinoAmerican Books (Second Edition, 2015).

The Easiest Way To Learn Mandarin: Image Maps, Word Images, And Other Mnemonics. SinoAmerican Books (Second Edition, 2008).

The Vengeance of Superior Men. SinoAmerican Books (Second Edition, 2015).

The Little Chinese Dreammaster. SinoAmerican Books (Second Edition, 2017).

The Bellingham and Gutierrez Crime Series. Gadfly Books 2015.

Chinese Short Stories. Gadfly Books 2015.

Crime With My Coffee: Stories, Ballads, Poems, and more with Joe. Gadfly Books (Second Edition, 2017).

Blues With My Crime: Facts and Fiction. Gadfly Books 2017.

ISBN: 978-1-943570-06-5 [Second Edition]

Library of Congress Control Number: 2017917757

Published by Gadfly Books (Glastonbury, CT, USA). www.gadflybooks.com

Notes:

- The unidentified pieces of verse or free verse scattered throughout the book and the "extras" at the end are taken from *Crime With My Coffee: Stories, Ballads, Poems, and more with Joe* or from *Blues With My Crime: Facts and Fiction.*
- Singular nouns in the mind maps and map lists (e.g., protagonist, killer, murderer, victim) may also be plurals; and examples given in parentheses are not meant to be exclusive.

This book is not suitable for children.

Contents

CRIME SCENE

Introduction

Mind Maps

Presentation: This book presents common features and options for 19 major facets of murder in the succinct, structured format of mind maps. For each of the facets, a map shows up to five tiers of features and options.

Purpose: The purpose of the maps is to provide writers of murder stories with a great number of detailed plotlines from which to create inimitable stories. To supplement this purpose, additional information is given in extended lists (e.g., common and uncommon weapons) and expositions (e.g., ranges, suggestions).

The maps are intended as a creative guide and are not alleged to be an exclusive catalog or technical manual.

Value: Although the individual features and options in each of the facet maps may be obvious, the map's structure may be less so. More importantly, all the maps combined allow users to quickly formulate any number of complete plotlines for evaluation.

Use: To create a plotline, the chosen story premise is used to select features and options as you go through the 19 facets. The same premise then becomes the premier source of ideas for fleshing out the resulting skeleton. The plotline maps can in fact be used to create new premises by moving through the facets with no preconceived plots and no favored killers, weapons, motives, and so on. Alternatively, you can browse the 100 story premises presented in "Additional Maps and Lists" to find ideas for new premises.

Remember murder stories can be either mysteries or not. To be a mystery, the reader can't know who the killer is, why he (or she) killed, how he killed, how he can be caught, or any combination until the resolution. While going through the maps, you can decide which features and options will not be revealed to the reader until the end or at all, as well as those that will be revealed earlier or later. In other words, the order of the maps should not determine the progression of the story.

Sample Plotlines: Three sample plotlines created from the maps are given in "Plotlines." Here is a simple murder plotline for a crime of passion:

1. **Protagonist**: Detective with a professional interest and law-biding attitude.
2. **Killer:** Lone, sane man kills once.
3. **Accomplice**: None.
4. **Victim**: Known to the killer (spouse).
5. **Motive**: Personal; victim known; crime of passion (infidelity).
6. **Plan**: Spontaneous, with little risk assessment (e.g., uses a knife instead of a gun); motivator is anger; subsequent reaction is panic.
7. **Site**: Spontaneous, with little conscious assessment—home considered safe; victim transported after the murder.

8. **Action**: Active killing; killer stabs victim; victim attempts to defend herself; both killer and victim are wild.
9. **Weapon**: Active; relatively fast acting knife; killer depends on greater strength.
10. **Injury**: Minor to the killer; fatal to the victim.
11. **Cover-up**: Before murder—none; during murder—improvised cleaning of blood; after murder—transported and buried body, threw knife away, returns home.
12. **Alibi**: Improvised because killing was spontaneous; waits a few days and reports wife missing; fears being caught much of the time.
13. **Detection**: Police investigate; crime scene unit searches house; wife's relatives accuse husband; neighbors snitch about abuse; no criminal record.
14. **Witness**: None for the defendant; credible hearsay that the husband is abusive; forensic expert.
15. **Evidence**: Circumstantial but cumulative: Wife's blood in the home, body found with stab wounds, kitchen knife missing, husband with no credible alibi.
16. **Arrest**: By police soon after murder; non-violent.
17. **Trial**: Evidence outweighs alibi; judge favors death penalty; defense pleads crime of passion for life imprisonment; media and public want death penalty.
18. **Sentence**: Aggravating factors (prior abuse) support the death penalty.
19. **Justice**: Criminal and moral justice served.

Map Lists

Items appearing in the maps are also listed as bullet points. The lists are redundant except for additional examples and comments and can serve as a different structural view of each facet.

Extended Lists

Data too extensive for maps (e.g., motives, weapons) are given in extended lists.

Expositions

The exposition of each facet supplements the facet's map. Where relevant, the range of extremes is identified—for example, victims can vary from the innocent to those deserving death as much as his or her killer. Examples and suggestions are also presented to stimulate ideas for unique plotlines. Because of the great complexity of every facet of murder in the real world, I present or reference few statistics (e.g., aggravating factors for first degree murder by state).

Additional Maps and Lists

Presented in this section are:

- map of a generalized story structure
- map of a pulp fiction story structure
- 100 original story premises
- 50 types of plot twists
- 50 types of story endings

A story structure gives framework and direction, a premise gives unity, plot twists give unpredictability, and the ending, whether satisfying or not, ends all the author wants to give.

Sample Plotlines and Samples Short Stories

In these two sections, three plotlines and three short stories are presented to illustrate the use of the maps.

Point of View and Definitions

Although I have included a map for protagonists, the point of view of the book is primarily that of an observer of one or more persons guilty of first degree murder. The following map shows how first degree murder is commonly related to other homicides across the United States.

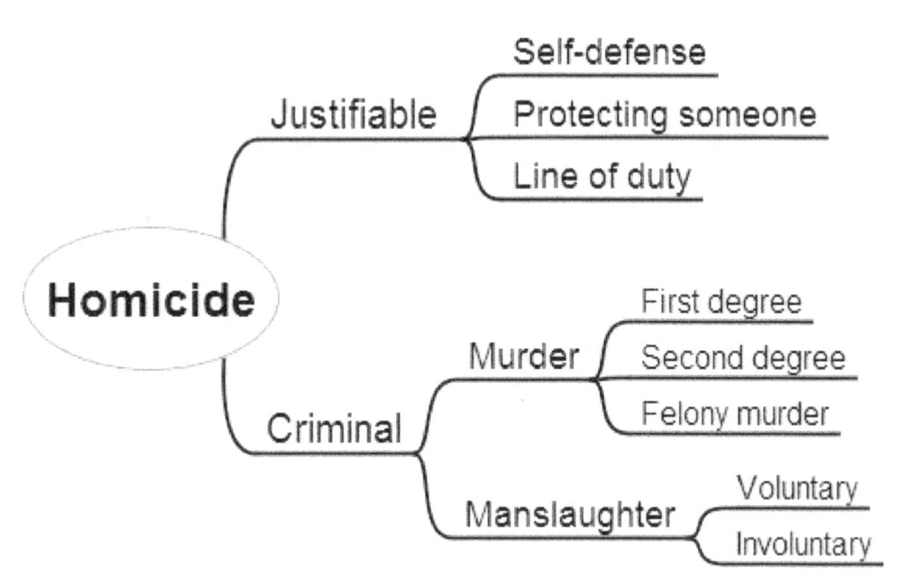

Homicide is an umbrella term for the killing of one or more persons by one or more persons. It may be justifiable or criminal. The most common justifiable homicides are killing to protect one's self or another person and killing in the line of duty by a lawful agent. Justifiable homicide is not a legal charge. Criminal homicide can be murder or manslaughter (also called third degree murder in some states).

In the United States, definitions of the various forms of criminal homicide vary among the states. The definitions given here are generalizations that may not apply to a particular state.

First degree murder is widely defined as the willful, deliberate, and premeditated act of killing another person. **Willful** means on purpose, that is, with intention. **Deliberate** means carefully considering whether to commit the murder. **Premeditated** means deciding to kill before the act. Because "depraved indifference" may be considered intent to kill, proof of intention does not need to apply to accidental victims. Deliberation and premeditation are judged to have applied if the perpetrator had enough time to change his or her mind before the killing. Some states do not require all three elements for the murder of children by unreasonable force, murder of a law enforcement officer, and murder associated with domestic abuse, arson, rape, robbery, and other violent crimes. Some states on the other hand require the addition of "malice aforethought," an evil disposition or evil purpose of the killer, for a murder to be classified as first degree.

Second degree murder is intent to kill without premeditation. It is most often a "crime of passion," such as the unplanned murder of an unfaithful spouse. In some states, acts considered so wanton or reckless death was foreseeable may be classified as second degree murder. An example is speeding along a crowded street. Unintentional killings during rape, robbery, arson, or kidnapping are considered second degree in some states and first degree in others.

When a killing occurs during a felony, participants who did not directly cause the death may be charged with **felony murder**. The charge may apply even if the death was unintentional. The victim may be the target of the felony, a bystander, co-felon, or fetus. Most felony murders occur during robberies. In some states, the penalty is the same as first degree murder.

Manslaughter is the unplanned killing of another person. Although voluntary manslaughter is usually intentional, there is evidence of "adequate provocation," a situation that incites a sudden and intense passion (e.g., anger, fright). Involuntary manslaughter lacks intention and results from careless behavior or criminal negligence, such as causing a fatal car accident while texting.

Depraved indifference, also called "depraved-heart murder," may be considered first degree, second degree, or manslaughter depending on the state and many case-specific factors.

An Overview of Murder

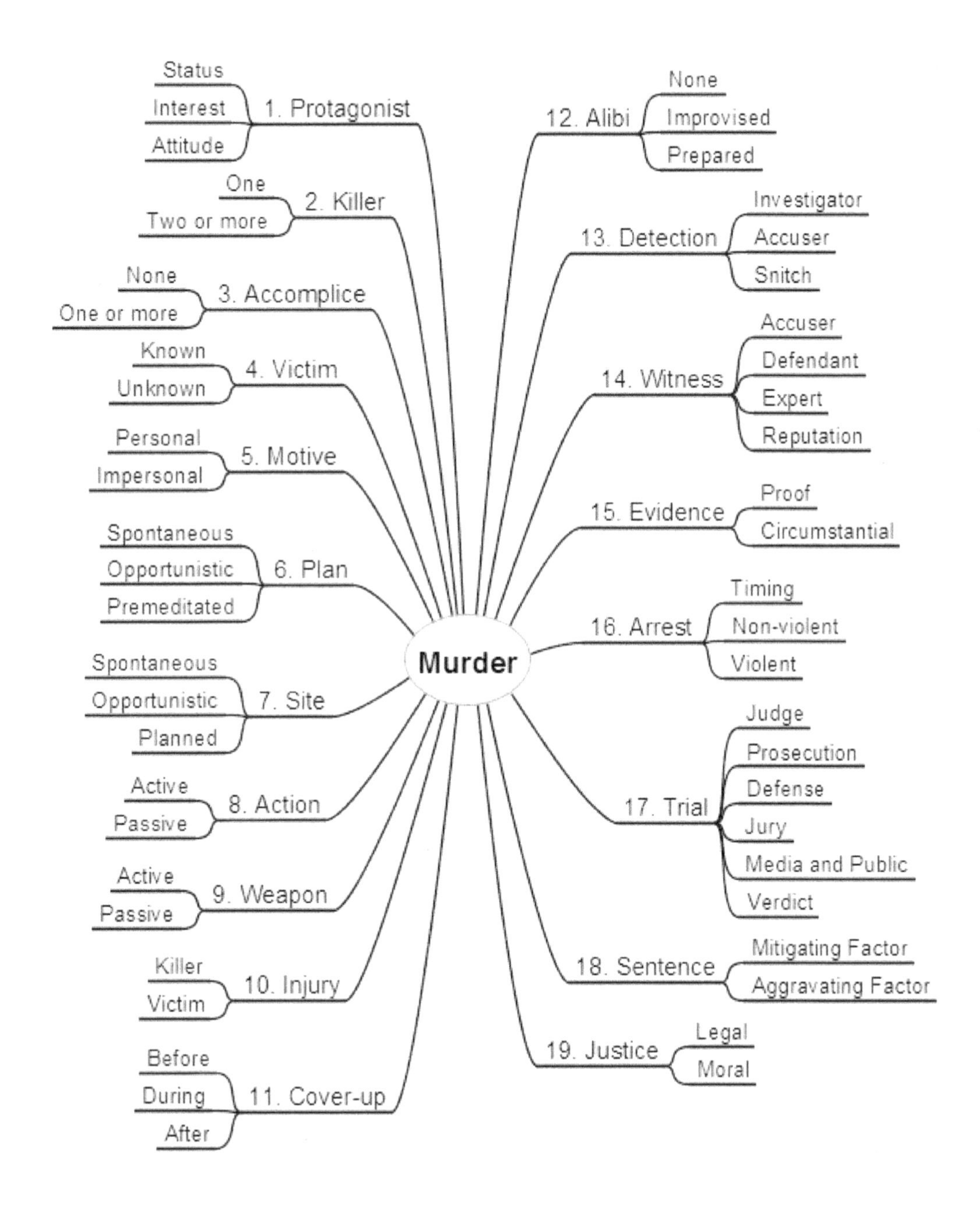

Exposition

Murder is a complex affair before, during, and after the act. By necessity, every story must focus on some facets strongly, some weakly, and some not at all. A story's premise determines which primary features are added and which are deleted. For example, a story of revenge and counter-revenge needs detailed histories of the killer and victim but not the trial and sentencing if the survivor proves self-defense.

In 2012, 37.5% of murders in the United States were unsolved (Reference 1).

Reference

1. Crime in the United States 2012:

   https://ucr.fbi.gov/crime-in-the-u.s/2012/crime-in-the-u.s.-2012/offenses-known-to-law-enforcement/clearances

19 Facets of Murder

* * *

"Even when she was dead, she was still bitching at me."

Serial killer Edmund Kemper

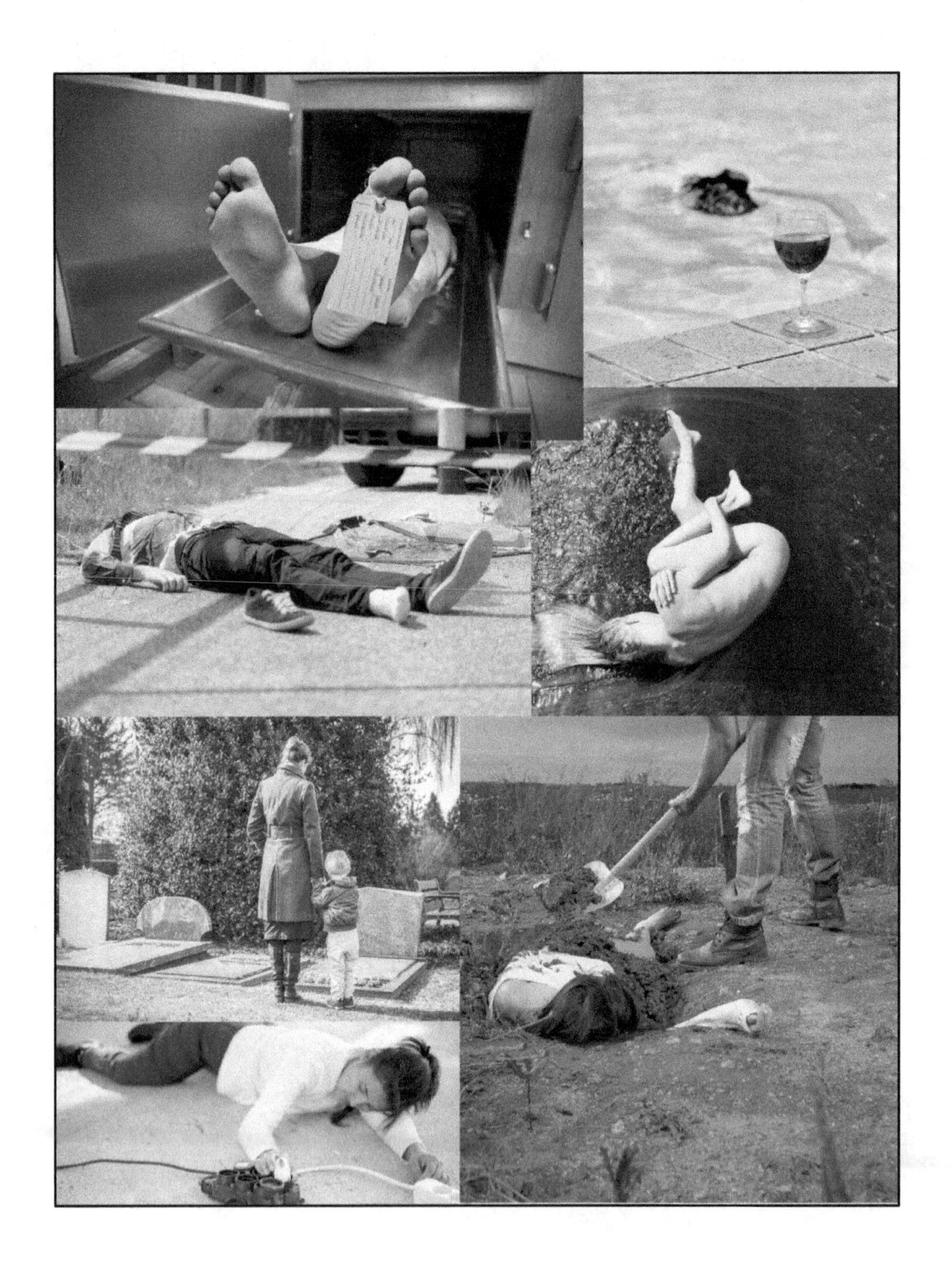

Facet 1: Protagonist

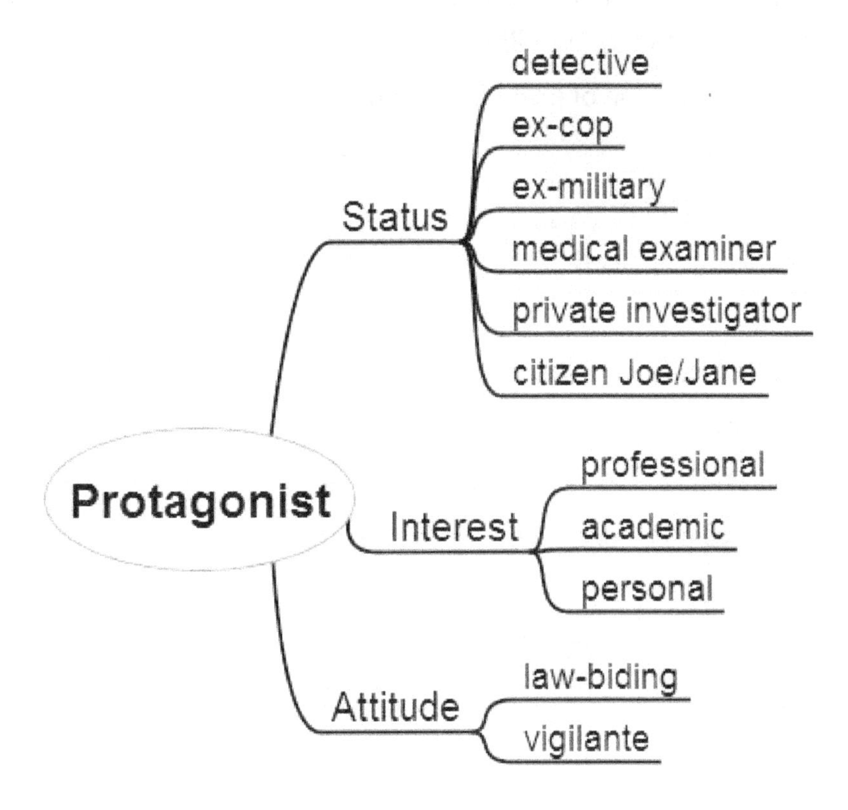

Map List

Status
- detective
- ex-cop
- ex-military
- medical examiner
- private investigator
- citizen Joe/Jane

Interest
- professional
- academic
- personal

Attitude
- law-biding
- vigilante

Exposition

By separating protagonists from killers, I am identifying the protagonist here as the villain chaser. The primary focus of the 18 other mind maps is on what the killer did, why, where, and so on. If the story premise places the protagonist in the fore, he or she must be injected into most if not all the facets to keep a meaningful presence. As well as status, interest, and attitude, the protagonist's skills (e.g., methodical, insightful) and traits (e.g., charming, abrasive, arrogant) must be shown directly or indirectly.

Here is a simple classification of protagonists and antagonists from best to worst.

1. Unrealistically good man
2. Realistically flawed man
3. Villain doing one good deed
4. Villain turning good
5. Spontaneous villain (e.g., unnecessary murder)
6. Opportunistic villain (e.g., rape of an irresistible woman)
7. Dedicated villain (e.g., murder for business)
8. One time killer who is also a rapist and/or torturer
9. Serial killer with no remorse
10. Serial killer with a passion for killing

Facet 2: Killer

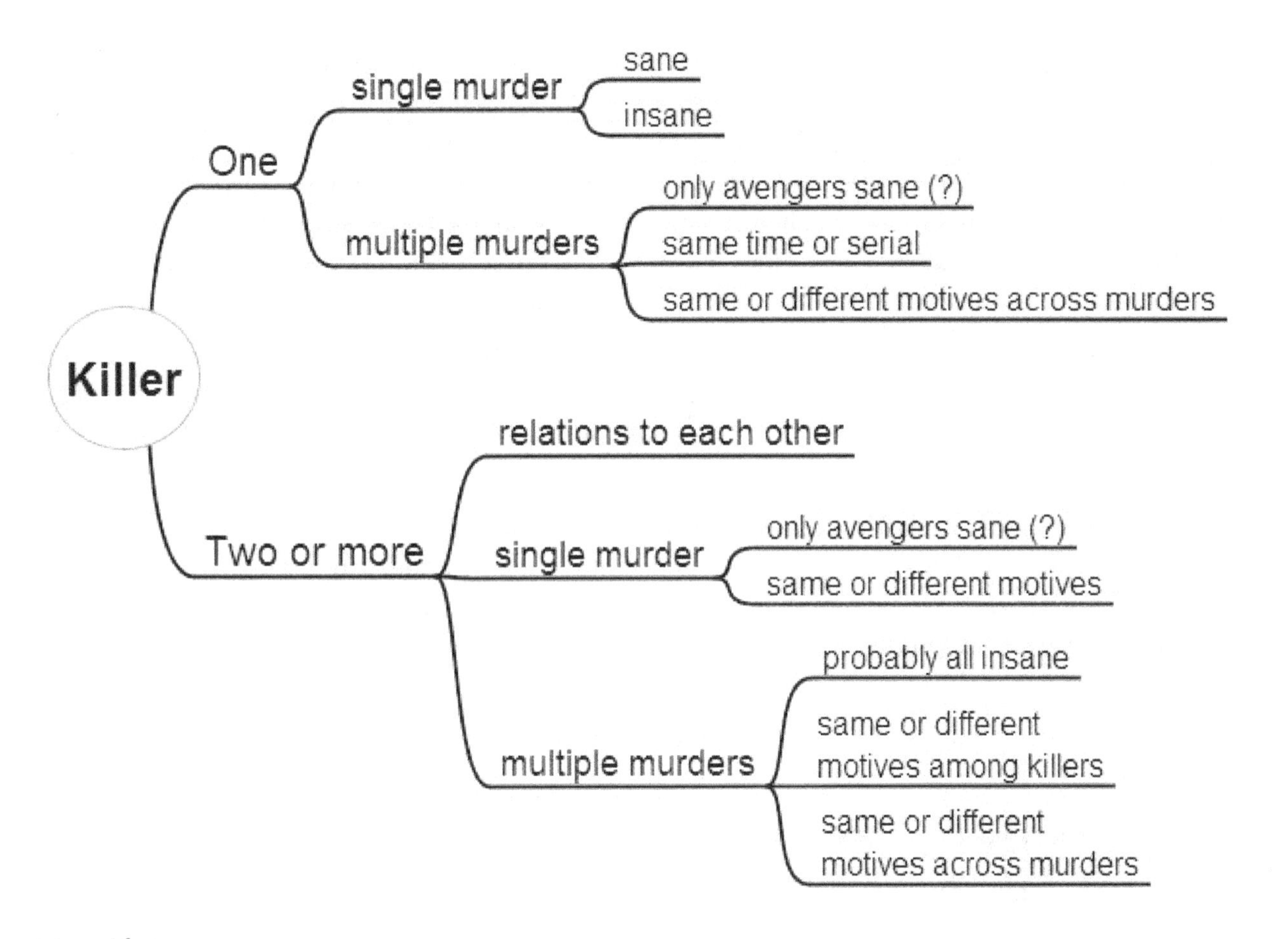

Map List

One

- single murder
    - sane
    - insane
- multiple murders
    - only avengers sane (?)
    - same time or serial
    - same (money) or different motives (money, sex) across murders

Two or more:

- relations to each other
- single murder
    - only avengers sane (?)
    - same or different motives
- multiple murders
    - probably all insane

- same or different motives among killers
- same or different motives across murders

Exposition

The chief concerns with murder are (1) the number of victims, (2) how the victims died, (3) the killers' motives, and (4) detection of the killers. In the US, murderers vary from a lone man or woman killing once to groups of men, women, or both sexes (families, gangs, gangster mobs, organizations) killing many times, though probably not in the hundreds—except of course for the Ku Klux Klan since its founding in 1865 and perhaps for the Italian and Jewish mafias during the 1920s, 1930s, and 1940s (Reference 1). The FBI estimates there are at least 35 to 50 active serial killers in the United States at any one time (Reference 2).

How victims died can refer to suffering (Facet 4: Victim) or the method (Facet 9: Weapon). Reasons for killing are covered in Facet 5: Motive. The detection of killers is considered in Facet 13: Detection. A list of the types of killings that normally lead to a conviction of first degree murder is given in Facet 18: Sentence (see Common Aggravating Factors).

Reference 3 gives tables for murders by age, sex, and race of both the victim and offender; and by weapon, relationship of killer and victim, circumstances, and more for 2012. For example, murder of a family member during the commission of a felony (e.g., rape, robbery, arson) is rare, while murder of a family member during non-felony situations (chiefly arguments) is not.

An FBI monograph on serial killers discusses classifications and myths (Reference 4). The myths include:

- All serial killers were raised in dysfunctional or abusive families.
- They are loners who are incapable of maintaining long term relationships.
- They increase the violence they inflict on the victims as the series progresses.
- They attempt to engage the police in dialogue and learn about the progress of the investigation by frequenting police "hangouts."
- Once a killer starts murdering, he can never stop.
- If there is a time break in a series, the offender was either in prison, joined the military, went away to college, or was admitted to a mental health institution.

Features of serial killers include:

- The predisposition to serial killing cannot be identified by any specific characteristic or trait.
- There are no combinations of traits or characteristics that differentiate them from other violent offenders.
- There is no generic template.
- They are driven by their own unique motives or reasons.

- They are not limited to any specific sex, age, race, or religion.
- The majority who are sexually motivated erotized violence during development. For them, violence and sexual gratification are inexplicably intertwined.

Reference 5 gives some additional classifications of serial killers.

References

1. American Mafia:

   https://en.wikipedia.org/wiki/American_Mafia

2. Serial Killers—How Many Are There?:

   https://www.creators.com/read/diane-dimond/01/12/serial-killers-how-many-are-there

3. Homicide data:

   https://www.fbi.gov/about-us/cjis/ucr/crime-in-the-u.s/2012/crime-in-the-u.s.-2012/offenses-known-to-law-enforcement/expanded-homicide/expandhomicidemain

4. Serial Murder: Multi-Disciplinary Perspectives for Investigators:

   https://www.fbi.gov/stats-services/publications/serial-murder/serial-murder-1#four

5. Serial killer classifications:

   http://forensicpsych.umwblogs.org/research/criminals/serial-killers-and-mass-murderers/

She committed the sin no wife should commit,
a sin no husband should permit.
She flaunted multiple lovers in my face.
Tell me, if you can, a greater disgrace.

I know a prison cell is being reserved,
but if justice was truly what *I* deserved,
I would be free,
for time served.

* * *

I blame the street preachers.
They always slipped out that "these poor bastards,"
men they would point to,
did it for a reason.
Fuck,
we all had reasons.

Facet 3: Accomplice

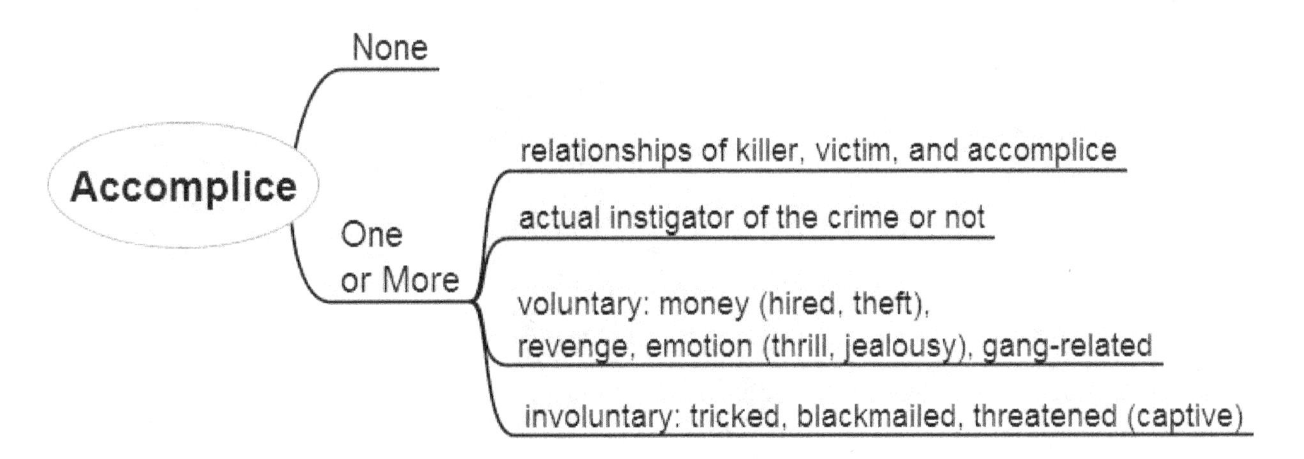

Map List

None
One or more

- relationships of killer, victim, and accomplice
- actual instigator of the crime or not
- voluntary: money (hired, theft), revenge, emotion (thrill, jealousy), gang-related
- involuntary: tricked, blackmailed, threatened (captive)

Exposition

To avoid excessive complexity, I identify accomplices to murder only here. Stories with accomplices need to include them in most of the other facets (unless they're murdered, freed, or escape). They can be the instigators of the crime, willing participants, or unwilling participants. Regardless of their relation to the murderer and the murder, they are bound to both and must be concerned with how careful the killer had been.

Facet 4: Victim

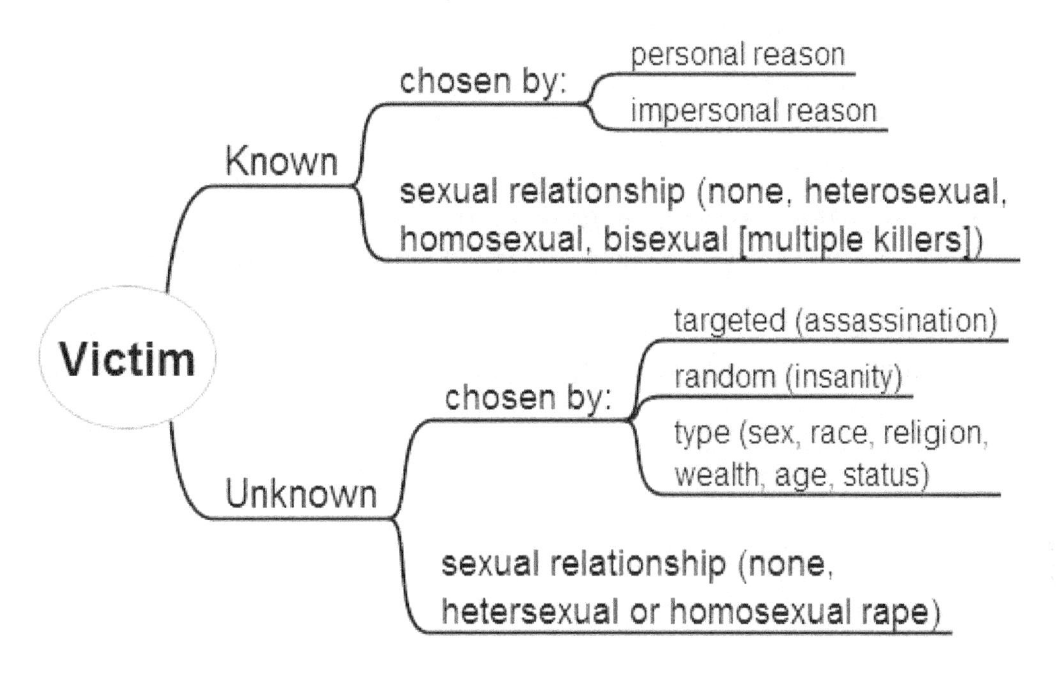

Map List

Known (by killer)

- chosen by
  - personal reason
  - impersonal reason
- sexual relationship (none, heterosexual, homosexual, bisexual [multiple killers])

Unknown (by killer)

- chosen by
  - targeted (assassination)
  - random (insanity)
  - type (sex, race, religion, age [hospital], status [teacher], wealth)
- sexual relationship (none, heterosexual or homosexual rape)

Exposition

Victims can vary from the innocent to those deserving death as much as his or her killer.

The relationship of the killer to the victim is a fundamental feature of murder because it has ramifications for most if not all other facets of the crime, certainly for motives, plans, cover-ups, alibis, and evidence. When the victim is unknown to the killer, how he or she is selected can be difficult to describe in a way satisfying to the reader. Because there is no mutual history, the "why" is in the head of the instigator, who may or may not also be the killer. That scenario demands creative descriptions of the selection and motives.

Reference 1 gives statistics for victims by age, sex, race, weapon, relation to the offender, and more for 2012. For example, one sniper attack occurred that year, by a man against his wife. Reference 2 gives statistics for hate crimes by bias (e.g., race, religion, sexual orientation), offense, victim, and more. For example, the FBI identified 1,376 victims of bias for sexual orientation of which 26 were against heterosexual victims.

References

1. Crime in the United States 2012:

   https://www.fbi.gov/about-us/cjis/ucr/crime-in-the-u.s/2012/crime-in-the-u.s.-2012/offenses-known-to-law-enforcement/expanded-homicide/expandhomicidemain

2. 2012 Hate Crime Statistics:

   https://www.fbi.gov/about-us/cjis/ucr/hate-crime/2012/topic-pages/victims/victims_final

Stalkers

Rejected stalkers want to avenge or reconcile
intimate relationships turned hostile.
The only solution is falling out of love,
the last thing this stalker would dream of.

Resentful stalkers perceive mistreatment, injustice, or humiliation
and want revenge as their palliation.
Acquaintances or strangers may be their prey.
Being the victim justifies this stalker's way.

Intimacy stalkers develop a perverted loneliness
that identifies non-existent relationships as harmonious.
Although love has not been earned,
violence may follow when it's not returned.

Incompetent stalkers live in loneliness and lust
through incompetence at building social trust.
They seek brief, false intimacy
because sickness or stupidity strangles sociability.

Predator stalkers are sexual deviants
invariably men seeking the sexually expedient.
Their stalking is a prelude to an assault
that lust for power and control make default.

All five kinds rationalize, minimize, and excuse
social skills they don't know how to use.
All five kinds possess a mentality
that's moving ever closer to bestiality.

Facet 5: Motive

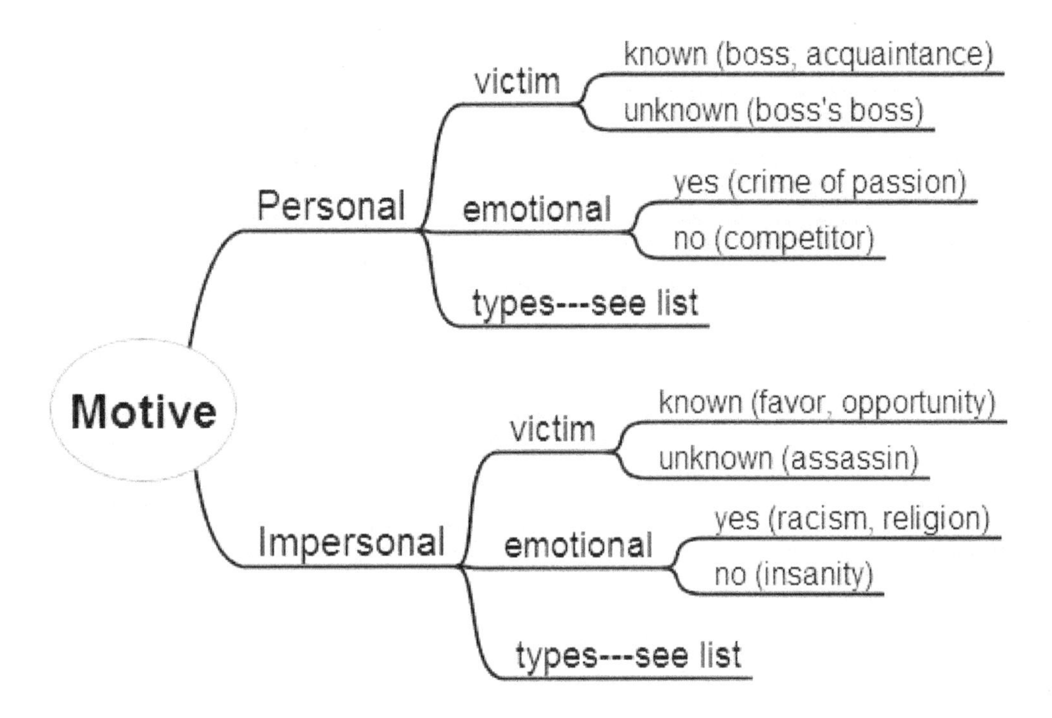

Map List

Personal
- victim
  - known (boss, acquaintance)
  - unknown (boss's boss)
- emotional
  - yes (crime of passion)
  - no (competitor)
- types—see list

Impersonal
- victim
  - known (favor, opportunity)
  - unknown (assassin)
- emotional
  - yes (racism, religion)
  - no (insanity)
- types—see list

Extended List of Motives (potentially impersonal motives are underlined)

1. hate (usually with delusions of superiority)
   - people
   - misogyny or misandry
   - race
   - competitor
   - individual or group
   - work, sports, love
   - religion
   - status/wealth
   - politics
   - class
2. fear (preemptive; real or imagined)
   - of being hurt or killed
   - of someone else being hurt or killed
3. silence victim
4. revenge (insult, theft, abuse, infidelity)
5. money
   - paid assassin
   - greed
   - inheritance
   - insurance
6. drugs
   - deal gone bad
   - incites murder
   - theft of drugs
   - debt for drugs
7. alcohol initiated
8. rape with intended murder (sexual aggression)
   - by men to women
   - by women to men
9. jealousy
   - promotion
   - sexual
   - money
   - friendship
   - fame
10. unplanned killing
    - after a rape
    - during burglary
    - during robbery
    - during escape
11. group-related (family, gang)
    - vendetta
    - ambition
    - defense
    - rite of passage or initiation
12. redemption for cowardice
13. pregnancy of wife, mistress, girlfriend
14. psychopathy
    - kinds: thrill killing, copycat, voices, blood lust, curiosity, power
    - genetic damage (mutation, bad mix)
    - physical damage (drugs, tumor, trauma, deficiency)
    - abuse, including bullying
15. freedom (abusive spouse, pimp)
16. replace victim (in a job, on a team)
17. escalated fight
18. rejection (love, job)
19. failed legal system
20. mistaken identity
21. annoying neighbor
22. nirvana/heaven
23. forced to kill
    - blackmailed
    - threatened or loved one threatened
    - tricked
    - brainwashed
24. obedience
25. excitement of an emergency (hospital

killings)

Exposition

Motives for murder vary from a sudden desire to kill during a robbery to anger intensified by years of conflict (e.g., work colleague). For these and every motive in-between, here is the deepest ugliness of humanity. Here is every depravity the mind can imagine and the body can commit. The problem is describing those depravities more than superficially. Motives are cans of worms within cans of worms. Is greed ever without jealousy? Is lust ever without aggression? Are there any extremes not attributable to insanity, temporary or permanent?

An exception to the label of depravity is revenge for a heinous crime personal to the avenger. Vengeance for the murder of a child is in fact widely commended. It is still inexcusable by law except when it takes place immediately; for example, a father killing the man who was killing or had just killed his child.

Reference 1 is a monograph on the motivations and behavior of serial killers. The primary motives are identified as sex, anger, mental illness, and profit.

Reference 2 identifies 10 senseless acts for murder (e.g., Columbine High School massacre). One researcher contends chromosome abnormalities trigger serial killing; and because the vast majority of serial killers are men the abnormalities most frequently occur on the male sex chromosome (Reference 3).

Reference 4 gives a number of observations regarding causality.

References

1. Serial Murder: Pathways for Investigations: [downloaded FBI pdf]
2. 10 Most Senseless Acts of Murder:

   http://www.criminaljusticedegreesguide.com/features/10-most-senseless-acts-of-murder.html
3. A Terrifying Glimpse into the Mind of a Serial Killer:

   http://www.businessinsider.com/12-shocking-and-twisted-facts-about-the-worlds-serial-killers-2012-6#a-chromosome-abnormality-seems-to-be-the-most-likely-trigger-for-serial-killers-1
4. Serial Murder: Multi-Disciplinary Perspectives for Investigators:

   https://www.fbi.gov/stats-services/publications/serial-murder/serial-murder-july-2008-pdf

I saw puzzles turned to paradoxes.
The biggest was
the music, dancing, and art,
all the best
standing against the crime, poverty, and racism,
all the worst.
Honey flowing down a canyon of filth.

* * *

The crowded, structure-filled streets
were not like the empty, open west.
Fast draw, slow draw almost never mattered.
Good shot, bad shot almost never mattered.
Ready guns, firepower, and close distance mattered.
But it was knowledge
the more you relied on,
the sooner you died.

Facet 6: Plan

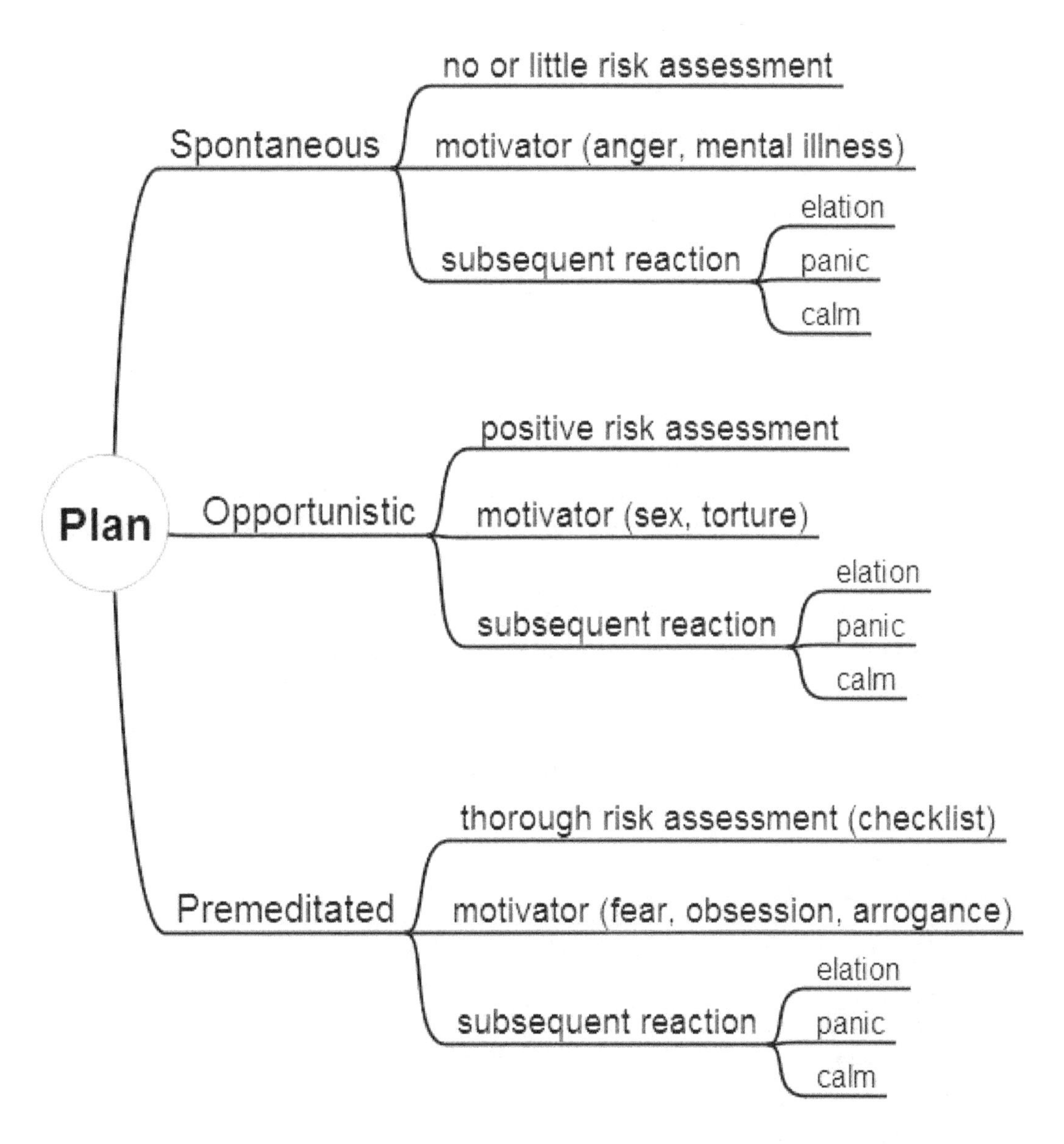

Map List

Spontaneous

- no or little risk assessment (emotional trigger)
- motivator (anger, mental illness)
- subsequent reaction
  - elation
  - panic
  - calm

Opportunistic

- positive risk assessment

- motivator (sex, torture)
- subsequent reaction
  - elation
  - panic
  - calm

Premeditated

- thorough risk assessment (checklist)
- motivator (fear, obsession, arrogance, jealousy)
- subsequent reaction
  - elation
  - panic
  - calm

Exposition

Time spent planning for a murder can vary from seconds to years. The would-be killer's emotional state and intelligence determine whether the act is spontaneous, opportunistic, or premeditated.

Spontaneous killers are emotionally driven, naturally or by drugs or alcohol. A study of 153 murderers found the third who were spontaneous domestic killers had more severe mental illness, fewer felony convictions, less intelligence, and greater cognitive impairment (Reference 1). The authors suggest spontaneous domestic homicide may represent a discernible criminological type. Impulsive killers more often violate parole conditions than premeditated killers (Reference 2).

Opportunistic killers are most often motivated by sex, though some are motivated by a desire to torture victims (Reference 3).

Premeditated killers kill on purpose, after careful consideration, and after making the decision to act. In other words, they commit murder in the first degree. Their plans can still vary from the cursory to the methodical. Cursory plans may account for no more than how to accomplish the murder successfully, while methodical plans account for detection and capture as well as success. Premeditated killers may be more intelligent on average than spontaneous or opportunistic killers, but probably still show a range in intelligence from the least prepared to the most prepared. It takes intelligence to keep impatience in check as well as to craft a good plan.

References

1. Hanlon, RE, et al. Domestic Homicide: Neuropsychological Profiles of Murderers Who Kill Family Members and Intimate Partners. *Journal of Forensic Sciences.* August 2015

   http://onlinelibrary.wiley.com/doi/10.1111/1556-4029.12908/full

2. Alfred B. Jr. Heilbrun, Lynn C. Heilbrun, Kim L. Heilbrun. Impulsive and Premeditated Homicide: An Analysis of Subsequent Parole Risk of the Murderer. *J. Crim. L. & Criminology*

108 (1978)

3. William M. Hamening. Serial Killers: The Psychosocial Development of Humanity's Worst Offenders. 2014

CRIME SCENE DO NOT CROSS

Facet 7: Site

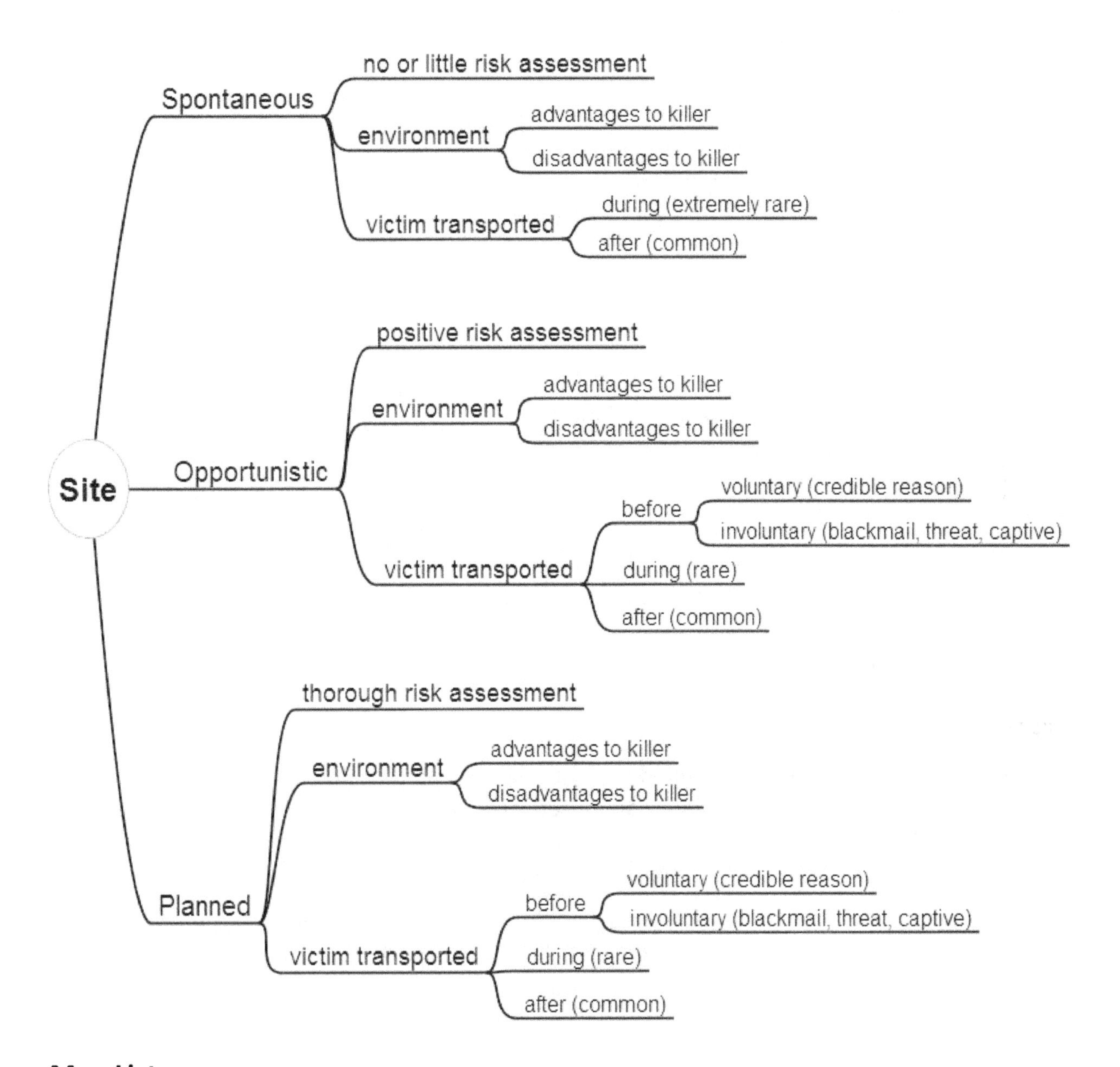

Map List

Spontaneous

- no or little risk assessment (emotional trigger)
- environment
  - time and location advantages to killer
  - time and location disadvantages to killer
- victim transported
  - during (extremely rare)
  - after (common)

Opportunistic

- positive risk assessment
- environment
    - time and location advantages to killer
    - time and location disadvantages to killer
- victim transported
    - before
        - voluntary (credible reason)
        - involuntary (blackmail, threat, captive)
    - during (rare)
    - after (common)

Planned

- thorough risk assessment
- environment
    - time and location advantages to killer
    - time and location disadvantages to killer
- victim transported
    - before
        - voluntary (credible reason)
        - involuntary (blackmail, threat, captive)
    - during (rare)
    - after (common)

Exposition

Crimes of passion and unintended killings after a rape or during a robbery occur at spontaneously chosen sites. Murders committed only when certain times and locations are favorable, such as during a vacation (e.g., boat, cliff), occur at sites chosen opportunistically. Murders at appointed times and locations occur at planned sites.

Investigators also classify sites by whether the killer attacked from inside or outside the chosen site (Reference 1); and whether the killing occurred indoors, outdoors, or within a conveyance (Reference 2). Reference 3 classifies treatment of the body after the murder, whether transported (dumped or concealed) or not (left "as is," displayed, or concealed). Where the body is found is considered the primary crime scene, though it is not necessarily where the murder occurred.

The location of the murder may have little or considerable influence on the act. Screams from victims and noises from bashing, beating, and shooting make most sites highly risky. The killer has more options in weapons and time, if not location, in a secluded building than in an apartment. Countless numbers of photographs of crime scenes with or without victims are available on the Internet.

References

1. Crime Scene Classification:
   http://www.inf.ufpr.br/lesoliveira/download/SAC2008b.pdf
2. Types of Crime Scenes:
   http://www.all-about-forensic-science.com/types-of-crime-scene.html
3. Serial Murder: Pathways for Investigations: [downloaded FBI pdf]

I stepped on his right foot and kept it pinned.
After sweeping his arms aside, I struck him on the chin.
I punched the solar plexus on his chest,
which left him too breathless to protest or confess.

I released his foot, pulled my hands back left over right,
and gave him a palm strike with considerable might.
The back of his head crashed against a wall.
It left a trail of blood marking his fall.

* * *

There were preachers, pimps, dealers, gamblers, thieves,
grifters, men and women whores, ex-cons, peddlers, drifters...
Every kind of lowlife
desperate for something,
money, food, sex, drugs, music, religion, retribution,
and possibly the unnameable and unthinkable.

Facet 8: Action

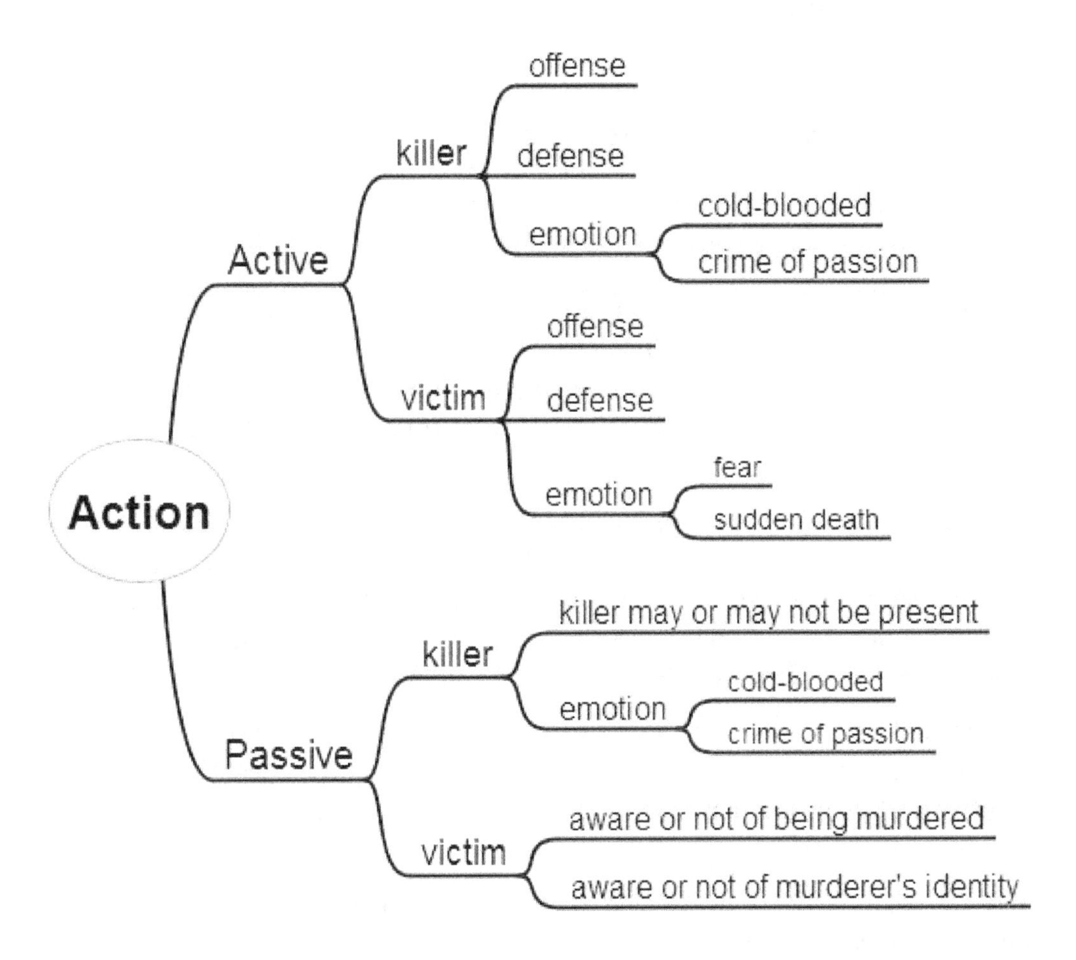

Map List

Active killing

- killer
    - offense
    - defense
    - emotion
        - cold-blooded
        - crime of passion
- victim
    - offense
    - defense
    - emotion
        - fear
        - sudden death

Passive killing

- killer

        - may be present (usually not alone with victim) or not
        - emotion
            - cold-blooded
            - crime of passion
    - victim
        - aware or not of being murdered
        - aware or not of murderer's identity

Exposition

Here is where the murderer's murderous actions are described. They may vary from tampering with a drink to torturing the victim to death. Facets 2 (Killer), 4 (Victim), 6 (Plan), 7 (Site), 9 (Weapon), 10 (Injury), and 11 (Cover-up) are fundamental elements of the act. Facet 5 (Motive) may be included here (e.g., rape and torture reflecting sexual aggression) or not (e.g., simple shooting).

The offense of the killer and defense of the victim will depend heavily on the type of weapon but may also depend on their physical attributes and the site. A victim may have no chance of defense or escape from an ambush shooting but a good chance to fight back and escape from a fist attack. And unless the killer is intimately familiar with the site, it is probably always more restrictive in movements, visibility, and sound than imagined.

The emotional states of killers during attacks may differ greatly. Both a poisoner and torturer want the same thing but one doesn't want to think about the victim and the other can think of nothing else; one is cautious and the other reckless; one is fearful and the other audacious.

A powerful killing scene can be tied to everything afterwards, most easily through the killer's memories or words. For example:

> *"I haven't blocked out the past. I wouldn't trade the person I am, or what I've done—or the people I've known—for anything. So I do think about it. And at times it's a rather mellow trip to lay back and remember."* Serial killer Ted Bundy

And of course the victim's fear is a highly dramatic element because it is difficult to overstate (with the written word) a woman's terror while being raped or a woman's or man's terror while being tortured.

Weapons are instruments of ill-omen.
[Daoist saying]

Facet 9: Weapon

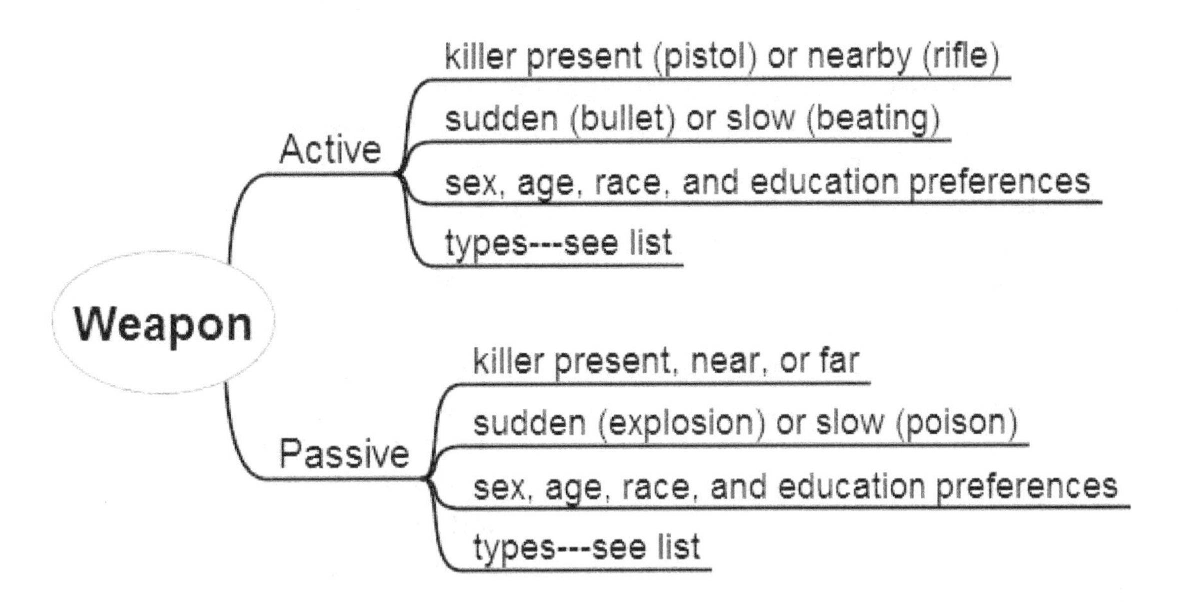

Map List

Active

- killer present (pistol) or nearby (rifle)
- sudden (bullet) or slow (beating)
- sex, age, race, and education preferences
- types—see list

Passive

- killer present (not alone with victim), near, or far
- sudden (explosion) or slow (poison)
- sex, race, age, and education preferences
- types—see list

Extended List of Weapons (potentially passive weapons are underlined)

10 Most Common (Reference 1)

1. firearms (primarily pistols)
2. knives or cutting instruments (axes, screwdrivers)
3. personal weapons (fists, feet)
4. blunt objects (hammer, bat)
5. asphyxiation
6. strangulation
7. <u>fire</u>
8. narcotics
9. drowning (primarily children)
10. <u>poison</u>

Uncommon (unranked)

- bashing
  - guitar
  - prosthetic leg
  - bowling ball
  - vehicle
- stabbing
  - corkscrew
  - crucifix

- stiletto shoe
    - spoon
    - ice pick
    - nail gun
    - knitting needle
- poison
    - switched medicines
    - injected ricin
    - toxin on a condom
    - poisoned toothpick
    - ethylene glycol in soft drink
- forced suicide (bullying, torment)
- slicing (sword)
- air injected into veins
- strangulation by belt or rope
- decapitation
- hanging
- suffocation
    - exhaust fumes
    - smothering with body
    - gas fumes
    - plastic bag
    - enclosure
- radiation poisoning
- car bombing
- pushing
    - off bridge, building, or mountain
    - into stabbing or cutting object (glass door)
    - into moving vehicle (car, truck, train)
    - out of a moving vehicle (car, truck, train, plane)
- exposure
    - abandoned outside
    - starved and/or dehydrated in a secluded building or bunker
    - locked in freezer
    - locked in car (heat prostration)
- torture
    - heart attack
    - organ damage
    - blood loss
- electrocution
- severed brake lines
- contagious disease (HIV by injection or sex)

Exposition

The great variety of potential murder weapons gives killers many options, including using more than one. By far, most involve direct action by the killer. Among the few that are indirect (including disguised and delayed weapons) are poisons (e.g., gas fumes, toxin on a condom), fire, explosions, contagious diseases, and traps involving electrocution, car crash, and exposure. Creating a credible alibi for a murder with an active weapon is invariably more difficult than for a murder with a passive weapon.

The greatest counter-advantages for forensic scientists are no two weapons are identical and no two uses of the same weapon are the same.

Reference 1 gives types of weapons used to murder, age of victims, and region for 2012 in the United States. For example, victims of 4 years of age and under are most often killed with personal weapons (e.g., hands, feet). Reference 2 identifies 14 everyday objects (e.g., carrot, pencil) used as murder weapons in movies.

References

1. Crime in the United States 2012: Expanded Homicide Data Table:

   https://www.fbi.gov/about-us/cjis/ucr/crime-in-the-u.s/2012/crime-in-the-u.s.-2012/offenses-known-to-law-enforcement/expanded-homicide/expandhomicidemain

2. The 14 Most Mundane Movie Murder Weapons:

   https://filmschoolrejects.com/the-14-most-mundane-movie-murder-weapons-7f1d2942bc58#.y1unzn2kc

She checked her pistol because one scar was enough.
She put it in her purse.
Would she be a philosopher or a nymph tonight?
Or more likely a philosophizing nymph,
because somehow many believed
she must be a wise slut.

Facet 10: Injury

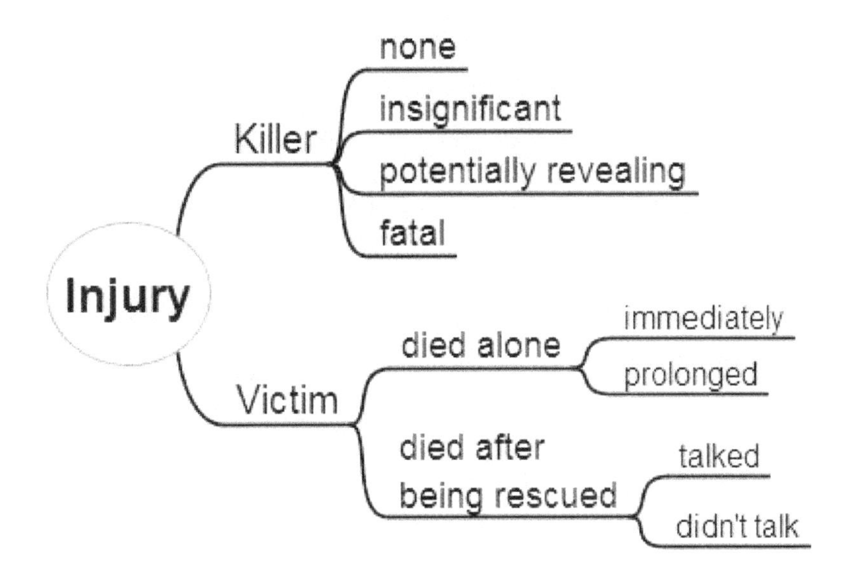

Map List

Killer

- none
- insignificant
- potentially revealing
- fatal

Victim

- died alone
    - immediately
    - prolonged
- died after being rescued
    - talked
    - didn't talk

Exposition

Victims can die with no pain or after a long period of torture. Undoubtedly most die with brief, intense agony (see Facet 9: Weapon).

Because of the long average length of time between a murder and an arrest, there is no way of telling what percentage of murderers are injured during a killing. Presumably a small number are, with few subsequently dying. Shooting and passive methods are among the safest for killers; while strangulation, beating, and bashing give victims the best chance to fight back. Even if the perpetrator is successful, injuries may reveal his or her guilt. A story in which the murderer died with the victim would require a great backstory.

A killer may be described as having remorse rather than physical injury, but the exchange is rarely satisfying—contrite villains can be as annoying as arrogant ones. A remorseless villain with a very good reason beyond insanity could be a better option.

So with curious eyes and sick surmise
We watched him day by day,
And wondered if each one of us
Would end the self-same way,
For none can tell to what red Hell
His sightless soul may stray.
[Oscar Wilde. *The Ballad of Reading Gaol*]

Facet 11: Cover-up

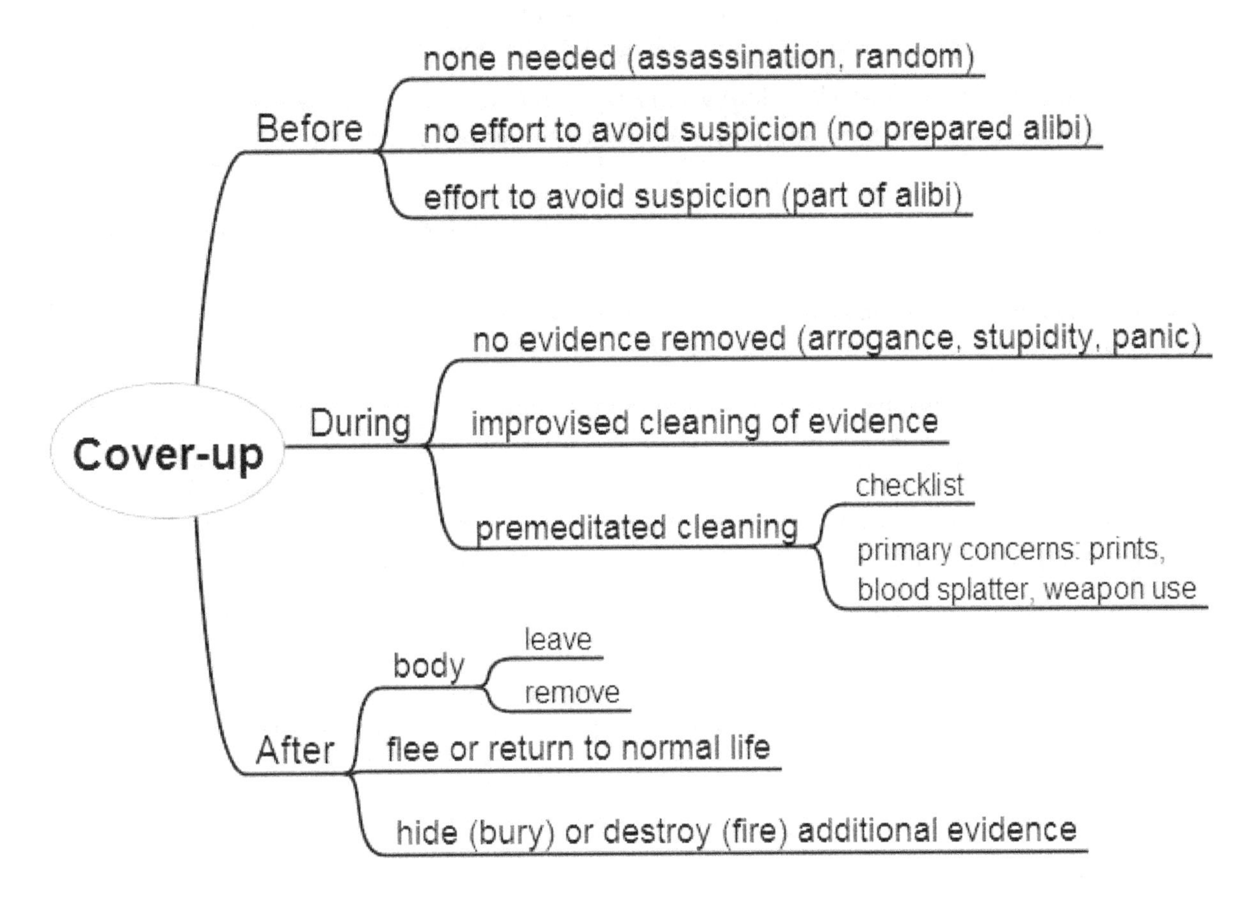

Map List

Before murder

- none needed (assassination, random killing)
- no effort to avoid suspicion (no prepared alibi)
- effort to avoid suspicion (friendly with victim; part of alibi)

During murder

- no evidence removed (arrogance, stupidity, panic)
- improvised cleaning of evidence
- premeditated cleaning
    - checklist (written or remembered)
    - primary concerns: prints, blood splatter, weapon use

After murder

- body
    - leave
    - remove
- flee or return to normal life
- hide (bury) or destroy (fire) additional evidence

Exposition

Cover-ups can vary from no efforts before, during, and after the murder to (1) careful preparations to avoid being suspected, (2) a thorough cleaning of the crime scene, and (3) a well-crafted alibi. A history between the killer and victim will influence the killer's efforts during every stage. If the would-be killer knows the intended victim, his or her preliminary schemes may include showing overt friendliness and broadcasting his or her intended alibi for the time of the murder.

Intelligence and emotion must often be in conflict during the act. One would expect the state of the murder to reflect the killer's intelligence; and that may be so for cold-blooded killers. For most, some degree of their intelligence, no matter how bright or how dull, is probably blunted by anger, lust, hate, fear, and other emotions.

Whether the victim is left or transported depends (rationally) on (1) means, (2) how incriminating the murder site is, and (3) the risk of time and travel with a corpse. Whether transporting or fleeing, the goal is to be seen by as few people and cameras as possible. An indirect route may have fewer eyes but more chances of misadventure. Whether the killer carries or removes the weapon depends on opportunities for its destruction or concealment.

In an analysis of evidence tampering (Reference 1), the FBI determined evidence was destroyed or removed from slightly more than a third of cases. The crime scene was cleaned in a seventh. In half, offenders took no precautions to disguise their identity or avoid leaving physical evidence. In less than a tenth, the offender wore gloves; and in a few percent, he wore a condom.

* * *

Here are some actions the killer can take to minimize evidence of his or her involvement.

1. For DNA, leave none, clean any left with oxygen bleach, or choose a site where the killer's prints and those of many other people would normally be found.
2. Wearing gloves is usually a good idea, except (1) the outer surface can leave unique "glove prints," (2) the inner surface may retain the user's fingerprints, and (3) thin gloves can leave fingerprints on external surfaces.
3. For weapons, passive weapons allow the best alibis (but require the most planning). The personal active weapons of hands and feet don't need to be destroyed or hidden but can leave DNA and be injured.
4. The act should be committed away from the killer's and victim's homes.
5. The killer should be far away from the murder site by the time the body is found.
6. The time chosen should be when the risk of being seen traveling to the site, being at the site, and escaping is the lowest. Very early morning is often the best time for a quiet murder.
7. If its destruction is certain to prevent a link to the killer, the weapon should be destroyed at the crime scene or nearby.

8. The victim should not be touched to remove anything or to move him or her.
9. A trip or an event occurring at the time of the murder may provide a good alibi, especially if a credit card was used beforehand.
10. Escape should be as inconspicuous as possible.
11. The killer should return to his or her normal life and not talk to anyone about the crime, sober or drunk.
12. If arrested, the killer should declare ignorance or forgetfulness for as much as possible to avoid contradictions and discoverable lies.

Reference

1. Serial Murder: Pathways for Investigations: [downloaded FBI pdf]

I told the scumbag what me being a cop means,
that I am able to manipulate crime scenes
to make prosecutions certain or come to naught,
and commit any crime I wished without being caught.

Facet 12: Alibi

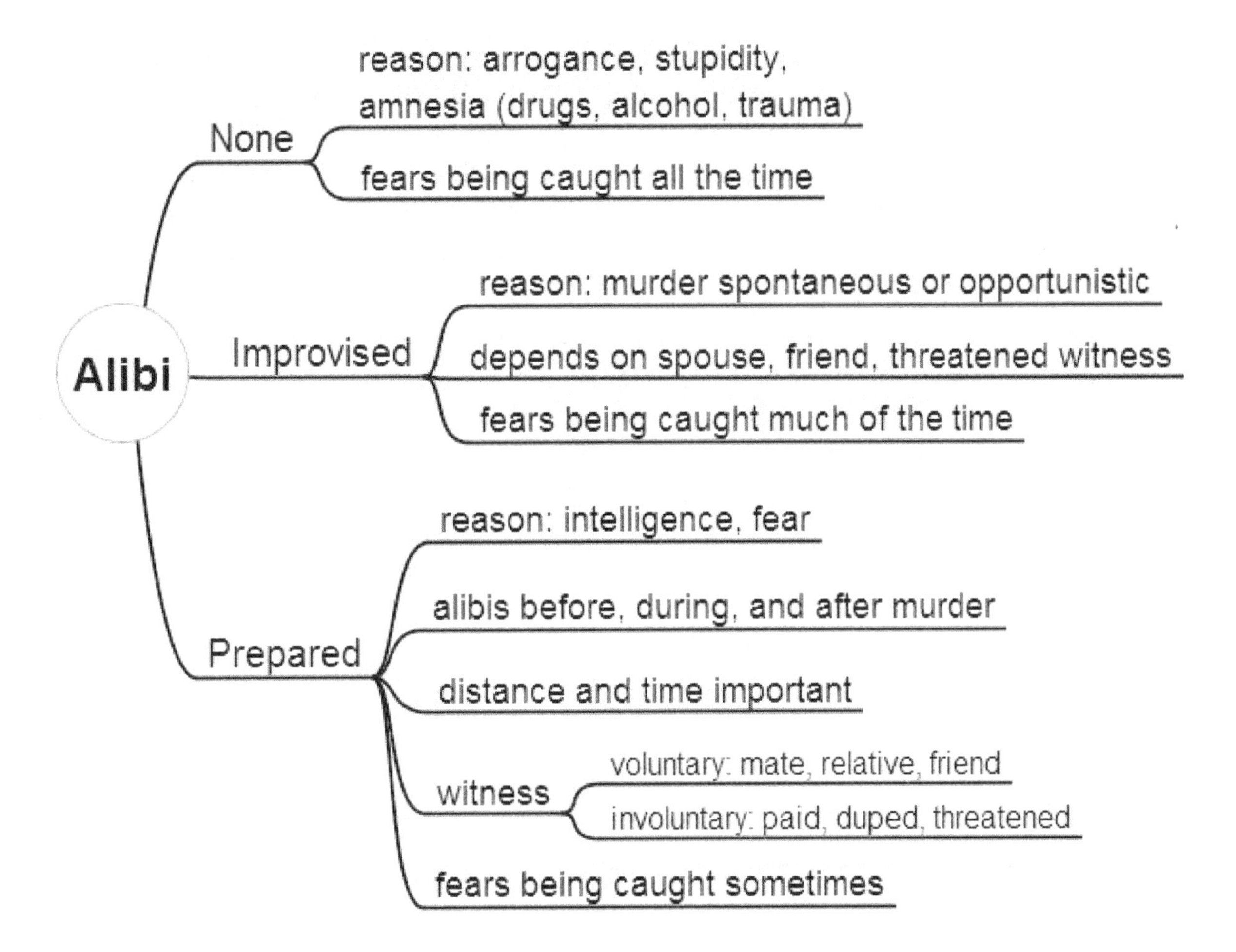

Map List

None
- reason: arrogance, stupidity, amnesia (drugs, alcohol, or trauma)
- fears being caught all the time

Improvised
- reason: murder spontaneous or opportunistic
- killer depends on spouse, friend, threatened witness
- fears being caught much of the time

Prepared
- reason: intelligence, fear
- alibis before, during, and after murder—"alibi times"
- distance and time important
- witness
  - voluntary: mate, relative, friend
  - involuntary: paid, duped, threatened

- fears being caught sometimes

Exposition

As well as none, improvised, and prepared, alibis can be classified as none, breakable by the police, and unbreakable by the police. If the killer's alibi is unbreakable by the police, it must be broken by someone else or an illegal form of justice must be imposed. Alibis can additionally be classified as based on documented support, witness support, or both. To manipulate evidence, such as phone photos or videos, the killer must be an expert or conduct research. For witness support, he or she may only need to be threatening. One solid witness is ideal, because multiple witnesses may become unwilling accusers as a result of inconsistent or incompatible lies.

A murderer's alibi is of course a collection of lies. "No, I didn't hate him. No, I didn't owe him money. No, I wasn't sleeping with his wife. No, I don't own a gun. No, I wasn't near the place he was found." During interrogations, detectives ask many questions and any inconsistency or contradiction in the answers will give them a path to follow—the more difficult, the more dramatic. When there is evidence against a suspect, he or she must lie away revealed evidence as well as potential evidence. He or she must face the necessity of corroborating all the big lies with smaller lies because detectives dig past what suspects claim.

Facet 13: Detection

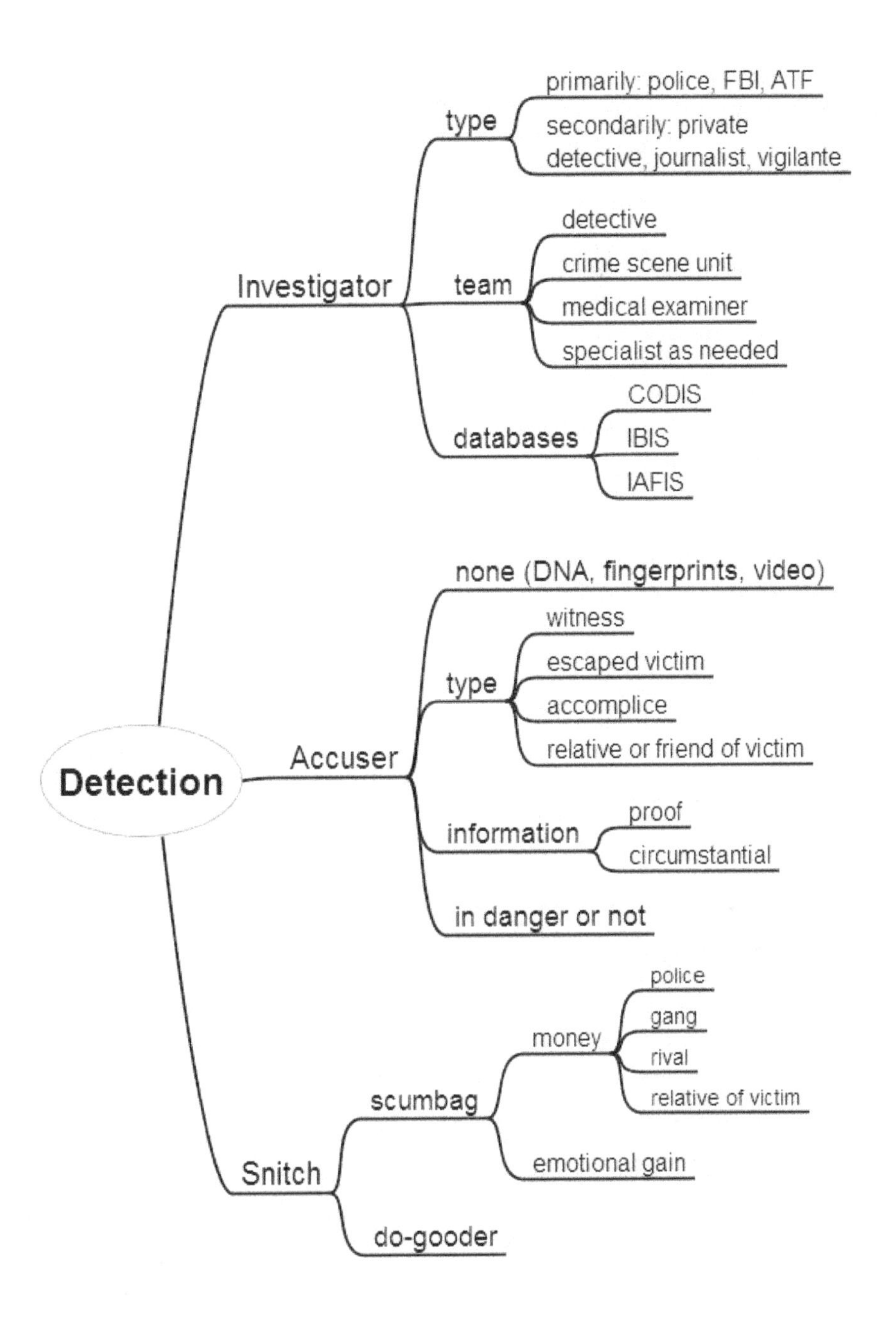

Map List

Investigator

- type
  - primarily: police, FBI, ATF
  - secondarily: private detective, journalist, vigilante
- official team
  - detective

    - crime scene unit
    - medical examiner
    - specialists as needed
- databases
    - CODIS
    - IBIS
    - IAFIS

Accuser
- none (DNA, fingerprints, video)
- type
    - witness
    - escaped victim
    - accomplice
    - relative or friend of victim
- information
    - proof
    - circumstantial
- in danger or not

Snitch (unnamed or anonymous)
- scumbag
    - money
        - police (confiscated money)
        - gang
        - rival
        - relative of victim
    - emotional gain (revenge, jealousy)
- do-gooder

Exposition

References 1 and 2 provide steps for criminal investigations. Reference 3 provides extensive information about forensic investigations.

Important databases for physical evidence are the Integrated Ballistics Information System (IBIS), Combined DNA Index System (CODIS), and the Integrated Automated Fingerprint Identification System (IAFIS). Databases important for networking among investigative agencies are the National Law Enforcement Telecommunications System (NLETS), Law Enforcement Online (LEO), and National Center for the Analysis of Violent Crime (NCAVC), which includes the FBI's Behavioral Analysis Units, Violent Criminal Apprehension Program (ViCAP), and Child Abduction Serial Murder Investigative Resources Center (CASMIRC).

There are many specific detection tools. *Shotspotter*, for example, identifies the location, number, and spacing of gunshots in the area covered by the system.

References

1. Investigators, the Investigative Process, and the Crime Scene:

   http://highered.mheducation.com/sites/0072564938/student_view0/chapter2/chapter_outline.html

2. Criminal Investigations:

   http://www.elearnportal.com/courses/criminal-justice/criminal-investigations/criminal-investigations-introduction

3. E.A. Murray. *Trails of Evidence: How Forensic Science Works.* The Great Courses Lecture Series.

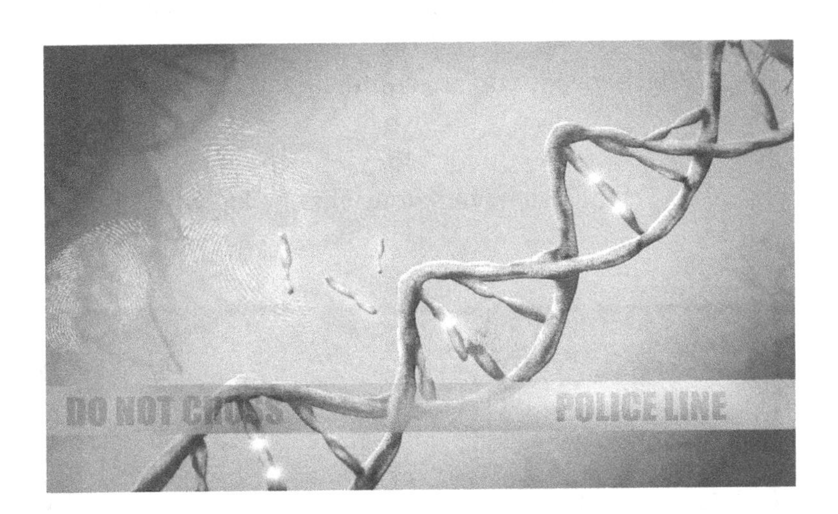

Spoiled Wine

"You gave your friend the bottle of spoiled wine?"
"Yes."
"Did you know it was spoiled?"
"Yes."
"Did you know it was badly spoiled?"
"Yes."
"Did you know it was spoiled enough to kill him?"
"Yes."
"Which means you are confessing to his murder."
"No."
"No?"
"You will never know what *he* knew."

Facet 14: Witness

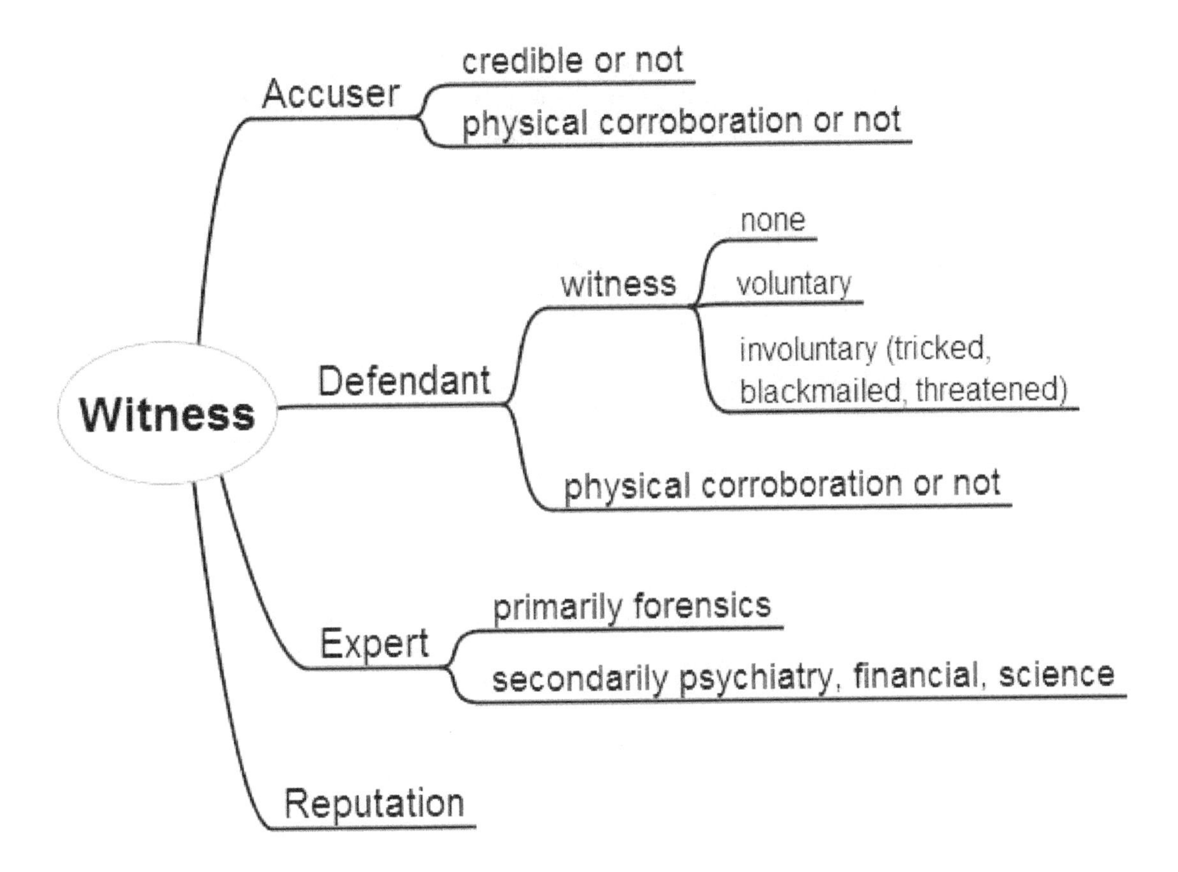

Map List

Accuser

- credible or not
- physical corroboration or not

Defendant

- witness
    - none
    - voluntary
    - involuntary (tricked, blackmailed, threatened)
- physical corroboration or not

Expert

- primarily forensics
- secondarily psychiatry, financial, science

Reputation witness

Exposition

A witness is someone who is believed by the prosecution or defense to have knowledge relevant to the charge against the defendant. Witness testimony can be voluntary or mandatory and oral or written. Witnesses are bound by law to appear at a trial when subpoenaed and bound to tell the truth under penalty of perjury after taking an oath.

Witnesses may be percipient, hearsay, expert, or reputation (Reference 1). Percipient witnesses are also called eyewitnesses because they testify what they perceived through their senses, aided or unaided by devices (e.g., binoculars). Hearsay witnesses report what someone else said or wrote. Severe restrictions on the presentation of hearsay testimony may apply in a murder trial but not for the arrest warrant or the grand jury.

Expert witnesses are professionals with specialized knowledge of some type of evidence. Reputation witnesses may vouch for or against the character of the accused. Snitches or confidential informants may provide investigators leads to a suspect but are not evidence witnesses.

For describing the behavior of witnesses or danger to them, References 2 and 3 may be useful.

References

1. Summary of types of witnesses:

   https://en.wikipedia.org/wiki/Witness

2. Do's and Don'ts—Being a witness:

   http://litigation.findlaw.com/going-to-court/do-s-and-don-ts-being-a-witness.html

3. Victim Witness Handbook:

   https://www.justice.gov/atr/file/782676/download

Sisyphus is more likely to be master of his thoughts
if not his days
by contemplating something deep inside himself
or many things outside,
rather than
his preposterous condition.

How else would you survive prison
and not go insane?

2. Left forefinger
2
3
4
6
7
10
12
14
15
16

Facet 15: Evidence

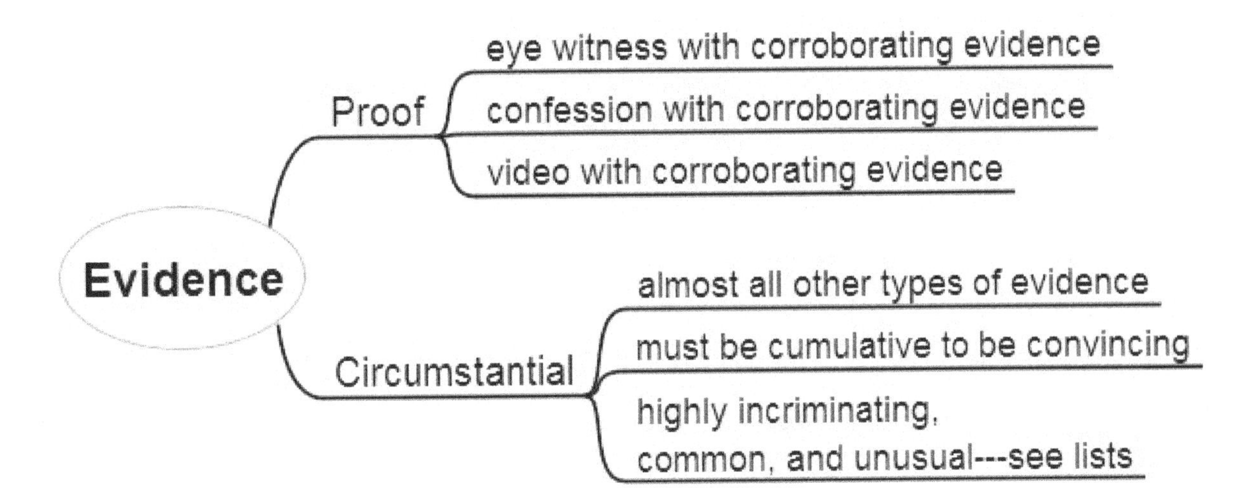

Map List

Proof

- eye witness with corroborating evidence
- confession with corroborating evidence
- video with corroborating evidence

Circumstantial

- almost all other types of evidence
- must be cumulative to be convincing
- highly incriminating, common, and unusual—see lists

Extended Lists of Evidence

Highly Incriminating Types

1. DNA (skin, semen, blood, hair, fingerprints)
2. Fingerprints
3. Blood (type, location, splatter)
4. Eyewitness testimony
5. Phone records (e.g., locations, texts, photos, contacts)
6. Videos (with or without facial recognition software)
7. Ballistics (weapon type, powder residue, bullet characteristics)
8. Personal items (e.g., ring, pen, photo, letter)
9. Clothing fragments
10. Hair (for analysis of DNA, race, drug use)

11. Soil and plant traces (for matching locations)

Common Types

1. Lies or contradictions to investigators
2. Resisting arrest
3. Motive
4. Previous threats
5. Credit card records (e.g., travel, purchases)
6. Overheard conversations
7. Social media posts
8. Suspect mentions information only the killer and police know
9. Tire prints
10. Stomach contents
11. Skin impressions from objects (e.g., belts, buttons, zippers)
12. Drug use (e.g., saliva, blood, and hair analyses)
13. Types of fibers (plant, animal, synthetic, blends, industrial), paints (automotive, structural, art), and glass (variations in density and refractive index).
14. Method of killing (to indict or eliminate suspects)

Unusual Types (Reference 1, 2)

1. DNA from an individual plant found at the crime scene matched DNA from seeds in possession of the killer.
2. Composition of lead in the bullet used in a murder matched the composition of bullets found in the killer's possession.
3. Idiosyncrasies of language used in written or oral threats or taunts.
4. Chigger bites tied the killer to the murder scene.
5. DNA on a toll ticket linked the killer to the time of the murder.
6. Pubic lice found at the crime scene and on the suspect.
7. Identification codes on beer bottles linked the killer to the crime scene.
8. Recovered "erased" computer files identified the motive of a killer.
9. Car carpet fibers and print of a rare tire linked to multiple killings and to the killer.
10. Use of cloth fibers to trace the movements of the killer at a crime scene.
11. Presence of sperm antibodies in the semen of a suspect who had had a vasectomy reversed.

Exposition

The first principle of crime scene investigation is Locard's Exchange Principle: The perpetrator will bring something to a crime scene and leave something behind, and both may identify him or her. In other words, there is always evidence. Another major principle is no two weapons are identical and no two uses of the same weapon are the same (Reference 3).

The common belief a person cannot be convicted on the basis of circumstantial evidence is not correct. In 1954, the Supreme Court judged "circumstantial evidence is intrinsically no different from testimonial [direct] evidence" (Reference 4).

References

1. TV series: *The FBI Files.*
2. TV series: *The New Detectives*
3. E.A. Murray. *Trails of Evidence: How Forensic Science Works.* The Great Courses Lecture Series.
4. Circumstantial Evidence:

   http://legal-dictionary.thefreedictionary.com/Circumstantial+Evidence

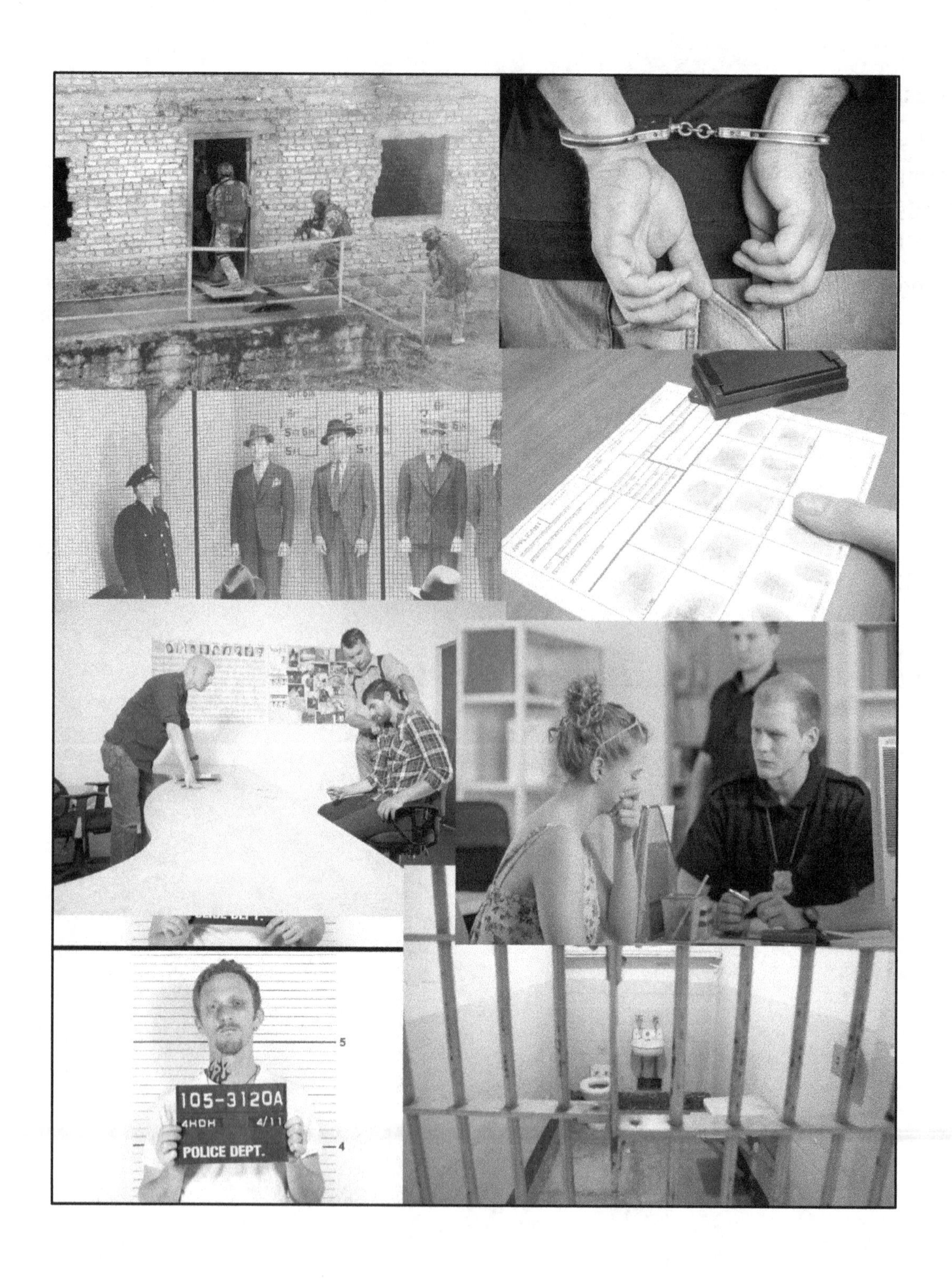
105-3120A
4HDH 4/11
POLICE DEPT.

Facet 16: Arrest

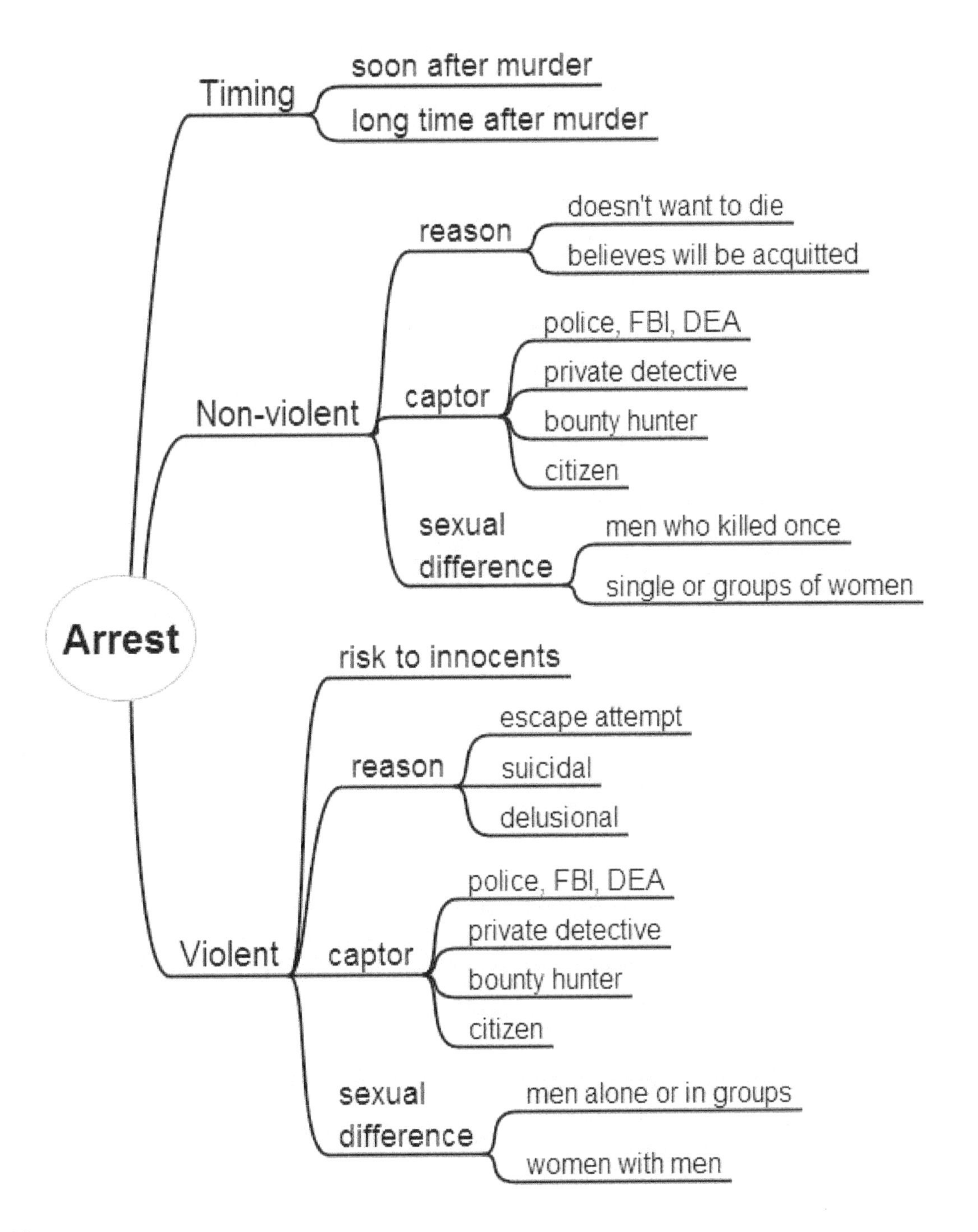

Map List

Timing

- soon after murder
- long time after murder

Non-violent capture

- reason
  - doesn't want to die
  - believes will be acquitted
- captor
  - police, FBI, DEA
  - private detective
  - bounty hunter
  - citizen
- sexual difference
  - men who killed once
  - single or groups of women

Violent capture

- risk to innocents
- reason
  - escape attempt
  - suicidal
  - delusional
- captor
  - police, FBI, DEA
  - private detective
  - bounty hunter
  - citizen
- sexual difference
  - men alone or in groups
  - women with men

Exposition

The arrest is a pivotal point in a murder story because the killer is in the hands of a legal system that wants him or her imprisoned for a long time or dead. Once imprisoned, a perpetrator is at a great disadvantage unless he or she escapes or is released (on bond or for insufficient evidence). That is why the period between the murder and arrest is often the whole story.

In the United States, law enforcement officers normally read the Miranda Rights to suspects during the arrest:

1. You have the right to remain silent and to refuse to answer questions.
2. Anything you do say may be used against you in a court of law.
3. You have the right to consult an attorney before speaking to the police and to have an attorney present during questioning now or in the future.
4. If you cannot afford an attorney, one will be appointed for you before any questioning if you wish.

5. If you decide to answer questions now without an attorney present, you will still have the right to stop answering at any time until you talk to an attorney.

However, the Supreme Court held in *Berghuis vs. Thompkins* (2010) unless a suspect expressly states he or she is invoking his or her right to remain silent and have an attorney police officers can interrogate the suspect, act on any information given, and use the information in court. Remaining silent alone is not an invocation of rights (Reference 2).

Not every arrested person is eventually tried. Indictments are dismissed for a number of reasons, including (Reference 3):

1. Lack of probable cause to arrest
2. An improper criminal complaint or charging document
3. An illegal stop or search
4. Lack of evidence to prove the defendant committed the crime
5. An unavailable witness who is necessary to prove defendant committed the crime
6. Loss of evidence necessary to prove defendant committed the crime

References

1. Chronology: The Arrest Process:

   http://criminal.findlaw.com/criminal-procedure/chronology-the-arrest-process.html

2. Berghuis v. Thompkins:

   https://en.wikipedia.org/wiki/Berghuis_v._Thompkins

3. Getting a Criminal Charge Dismissed:

   http://www.criminaldefenselawyer.com/resources/criminal-defense/criminal-defense-case/charge-dimissal-court.htm

Facet 17: Trial (Guilt Phase)

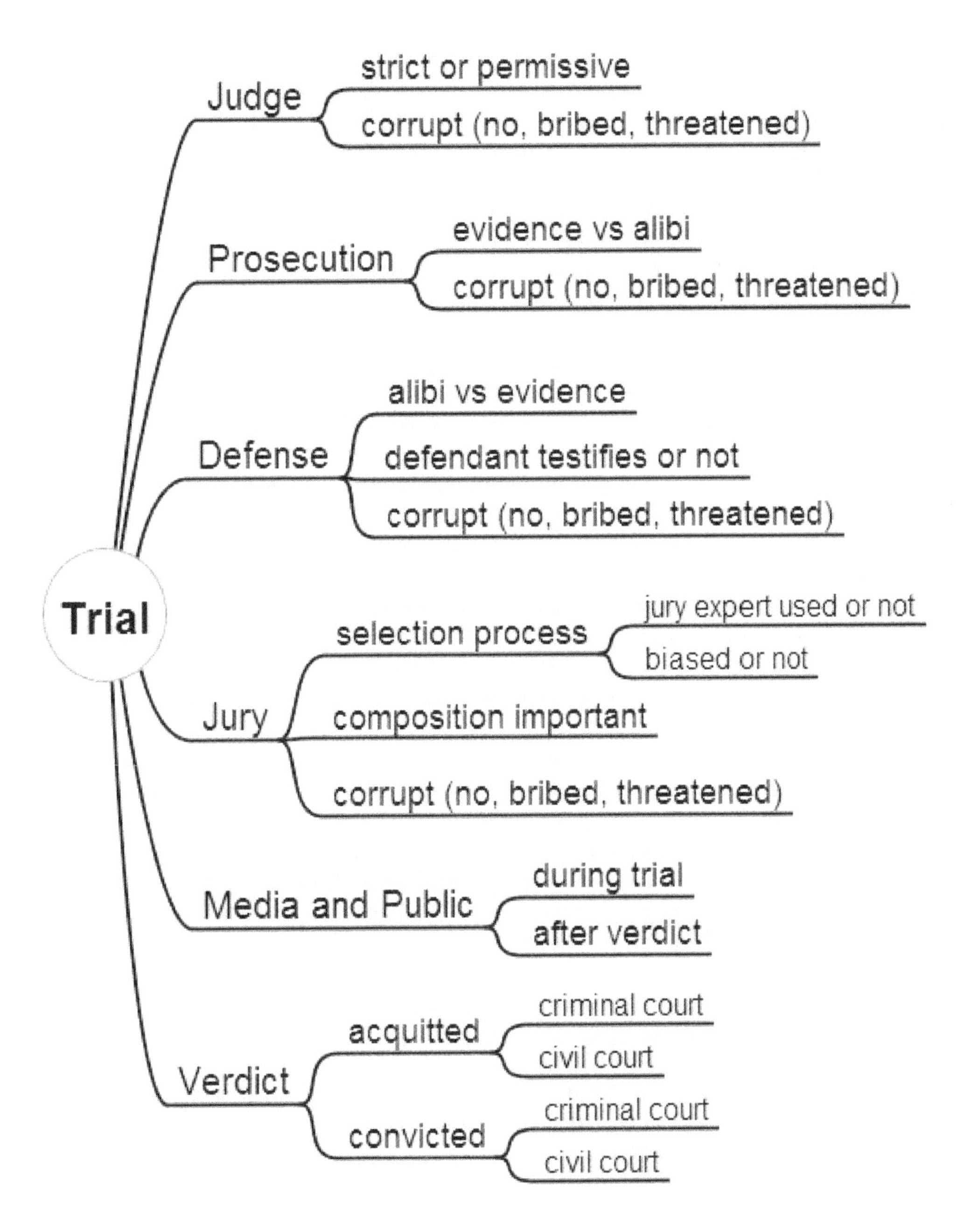

Map List

Judge

- strict or permissive (evidence, questioning)
- corrupt (no, bribed, threatened)

Prosecution

- evidence vs alibi
- corrupt (no, bribed, threatened)

Defense

- alibi vs evidence
- defendant testifies or not
- corrupt (no, bribed, threatened)

Jury

- selection process
    - jury expert used by defense or not
    - biased result or not
- composition (age, sex, race, background) important
- corrupt (no, bribed, threatened)

Media and Public

- during trial
- after verdict

Verdict

- acquitted
    - criminal court
    - civil court
- convicted
    - criminal court
    - civil court

Exposition

Capital cases commonly must pass through a number of steps before coming to trial (Reference 1). A description of a trial itself involves interweaving laws, professional profiles, evidence, motives, histories, events, and personalities for an extended period of time. Although states vary in what pleas are accepted for first degree murder, in general suspects may plead (1) innocence; (2) guilty of a lesser charge (second degree or manslaughter); (3) not guilty by reason of self-defense, defense of another person, or insanity; (4) guilty as charged; or (5) no contest (in a few states). Pleas other than innocence require proof by the defense.

A defendant's chief concerns about the judge are whether he or she is strict or lenient in permitting questioning and evidence and favors maximum or minimum sentences. Few suspects are able to corrupt judges by bribery or threats.

Whether the accused testifies can have a dramatic impact on the story. It has been contended juries have an inherent bias against defendants who testify. Defenses include mistaken identity, justified homicide (self-defense, defense of another), accident or misfortune, and insanity (References 2 and 3). Defense lawyers are concerned with the legal guilt of their clients, that is, what the prosecution can prove, and not whether the client is factually guilty (Reference 4). Even if they believe their client is guilty, they are ethically and legally (by not lying) bound to attempt to disprove the prosecution's case.

Juries have a high probability of bias if loaded towards one sex, race, or financial class. Negative bias most often occurs in cases involving male defendants standing against children or women victims and cases involving minorities. Positive bias most often occurs in cases involving the wealthy, attractive, or well-known defendants. The news media and public also have the potential for prejudice.

A criminal trial may end in an acquittal, conviction, or a hung jury. If the jury is not unanimous, which happens in less than 10% of trial cases (Reference 5), the prosecution may try again with a different jury, dismiss the charge, or make a plea bargain with the defendant. In the case of acquittal, the suspect may still be convicted in a civil court for violating the victim's civil rights. That court can impose long prison sentences but not the death penalty.

References

1. Flowcharts of the criminal justice system:

   http://www.americanbar.org/groups/public_education/resources/law_related_education_network/how_courts_work/casediagram.html

   https://www.nassaucountyny.gov/562/Progress-of-the-Criminal-Case

2. First Degree Murder Defenses:

   http://criminal.findlaw.com/criminal-charges/first-degree-murder-defenses.html

3. Insanity Defense:

   http://criminal.findlaw.com/criminal-procedure/insanity-defense.html

4. Representing a Client Who the Lawyer Thinks is Guilty:

   http://www.nolo.com/legal-encyclopedia/representing-client-whom-the-lawyer-thinks-is-guilty.html

5. Do Juror Pressures Lead to Unfair Verdicts?:

   http://www.apa.org/monitor/2008/03/jn.aspx

"Death fades into insignificance when compared with life imprisonment. To spend each night in jail, day after day, year after year, gazing at the bars and longing for freedom, is indeed expiation." Lewis E. Lawes, warden of Sing Sing prison, 1920–41

Facet 18: Sentence (Penalty Phase)

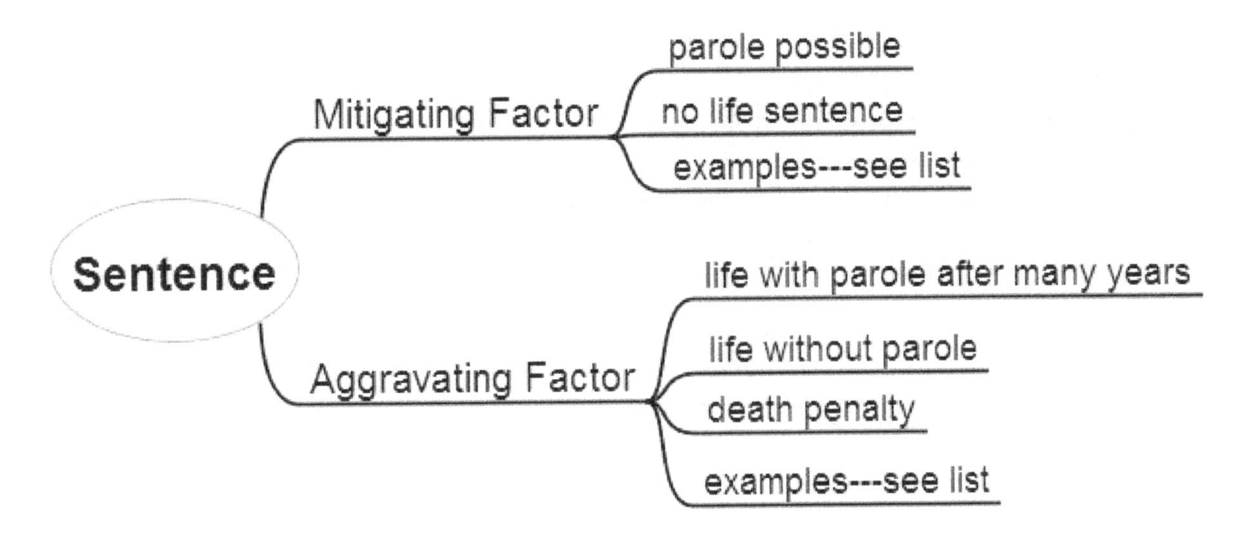

Map List

Mitigating factor

- parole possible
- no life sentence
- examples—see list

Aggravating factor

- life with parole after many years
- life without parole
- death penalty
- examples—see list

Exposition

In the United States, sentencing for first degree murder varies from state to state. In all states, both mitigating and aggravating factors are considered in determining whether the sentence is execution (in states with the death penalty), life imprisonment, or some combination of years behind bars and parole. These factors may concern the crime, criminal, or victim. In states with the death penalty, the sentencing agent, whether judge or jury, is not require to find mitigating factors to impose life imprisonment but must find aggravating factors to impose the death penalty (Reference 1). Most defense teams include a mitigation specialist.

Common mitigating factors:

1. No previous felonies
2. History of mental illness
3. Intellectual disability

4. Minor participation in the crime
5. Victim's consent to engage in the crime resulting in his or her death
6. Remorse
7. Addiction
8. Childhood abuse or neglect

Mitigating factors for capital punishment by state are given in Reference 2.

Common aggravating factors:

1. Multiple murders
2. Killing a child by unreasonable force
3. Killing a law enforcement officer
4. Previous felony convictions
5. Victim was tortured
6. Murder was committed to prevent arrest, escape custody, or conceal a crime
7. Murder was committed during commission of a felony
8. Persons other than the victim were at grave risk of death at the time of the murder

Aggravating factors for capital punishment by state are given in Reference 3.

After being convicted, defendants dissatisfied with their attorney's defense can declare "ineffective assistance of counsel." He or she must show the defense counsel's performance was deficient and the outcome was prejudiced.

References

1. Mitigation in Capital Cases:

   http://www.capitalpunishmentincontext.org/issues/mitigation

2. State Death Penalty Mitigation Statutes:

   http://www.jdsupra.com/post/documentViewer.aspx?fid=d61d8c7b-896b-4c1a-bd87-f86425206b45

3. Aggravating Factors for Capital Punishment by State:

   http://www.deathpenaltyinfo.org/aggravating-factors-capital-punishment-state

Facet 19: Justice

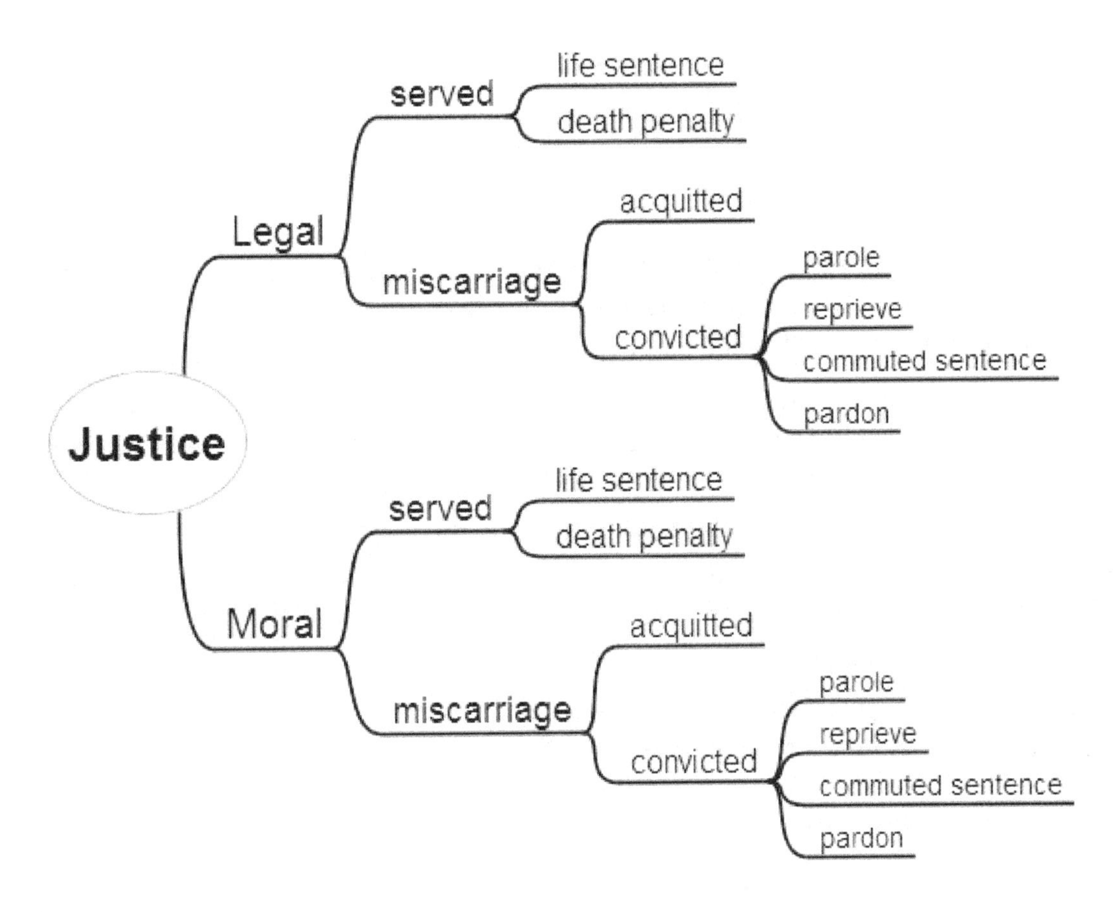

Map List

Legal

- served
    - life sentence
    - death penalty
- miscarriage
    - acquitted
    - convicted
        - parole
        - reprieve
        - commuted sentence
        - pardon

Moral

- served
    - life sentence
    - death penalty
- miscarriage

- acquitted
- convicted
    - parole
    - reprieve
    - commuted sentence
    - pardon

Exposition

The verdict in a murder trial should be perceived as serving both legal and moral justice. The outcome may appear to be only one or neither for a number of reasons, including extenuating circumstances, discrimination, mistakes, and corruption.

Clemency for a person who has committed first degree murder may be of several kinds. Among individuals and agencies with the authority to grant some or all of the forms of clemency are the President of the United States, State governors, and boards of pardons.

Parole is the conditional release from prison for the remaining sentence. Release may be discretionary (by a parole board) or mandatory (by statute). For example, possible punishment for first degree murder in Arizona includes parole in 25 years. Parolees must obey a number of restrictions on their freedom.

A **reprieve** is the postponement of a sentence to permit time for an appeal. Reprieves are usually granted because of new or extenuating circumstances. The nullifying of a death sentence is a commutation not a reprieve. Drama over the uncertainty of a last minute commutation of a death sentence is high but well worn.

A **commutation of sentence** is a reduction in punishment by the substitution of a lesser crime. **Remission** is the reduction of punishment without altering the conviction. A commutation or remission implies the penalty was excessive or the prisoner had been rehabilitated or has shown exceptionally good conduct. In neither are the felon's civil rights restored. Becoming or pretending to be a born-again Christian is perhaps the most persuasive way of showing rehabilitation in the United States.

A Presidential **pardon** is forgiveness of a federal offense. It implies the penalty was excessive or the offender has reformed or shown exceptionally good conduct. It is usually awarded after time served. The record of the conviction is not expunged. The primary benefits include public recognition of rehabilitation and restoration of civil rights, including the rights to vote and hold public office. In some states (e.g., Pennsylvania), a governor's pardon may completely nullify the conviction of a state crime.

Additional Maps and Lists

* * *

I was framed by things I didn't do.
I was framed by things I did too.
My life, like yours, has been a dance
between limited potential and limited chance.

...pulling a trigger requires no skill, no mental training, no code of conduct, and no courage; nothing more than the same muscles as a monkey.

Generalized Story Structure

Here is one of many possible story structures.

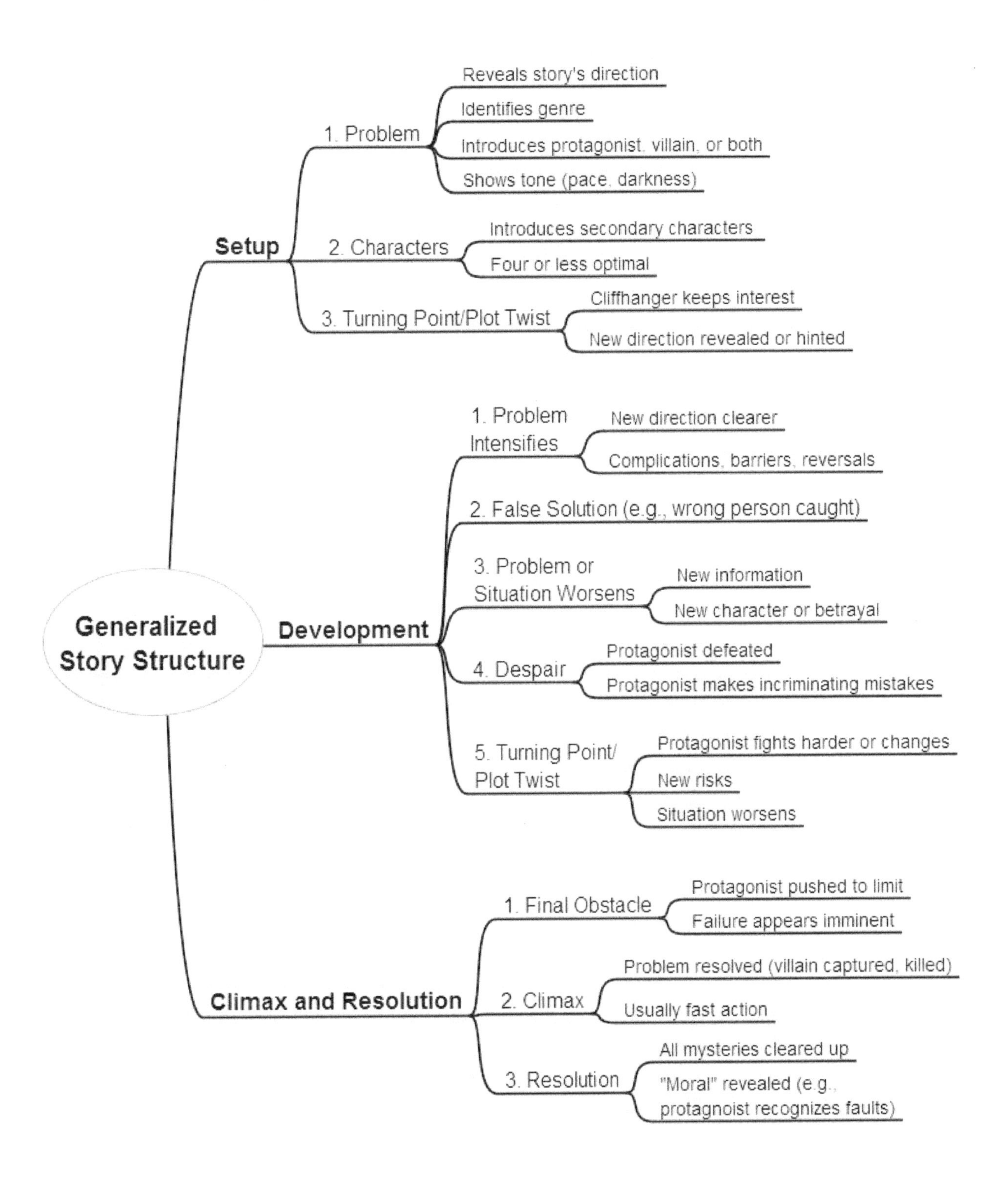

From her, I'm free
except for the poltergeist stalking me.

Every whisper,
every call,
every knock on the door
speaks to me of a life that's lived no more.

Pulp Fiction Story Structure

In the 1930s and 1940s, Lester Dent was the master of pulp fiction, with 182 Doc Savage novels alone. Here is the formula he used for his 6,000 word stories. The focus is on the frequent, nearly continuous misfortune of the hero.

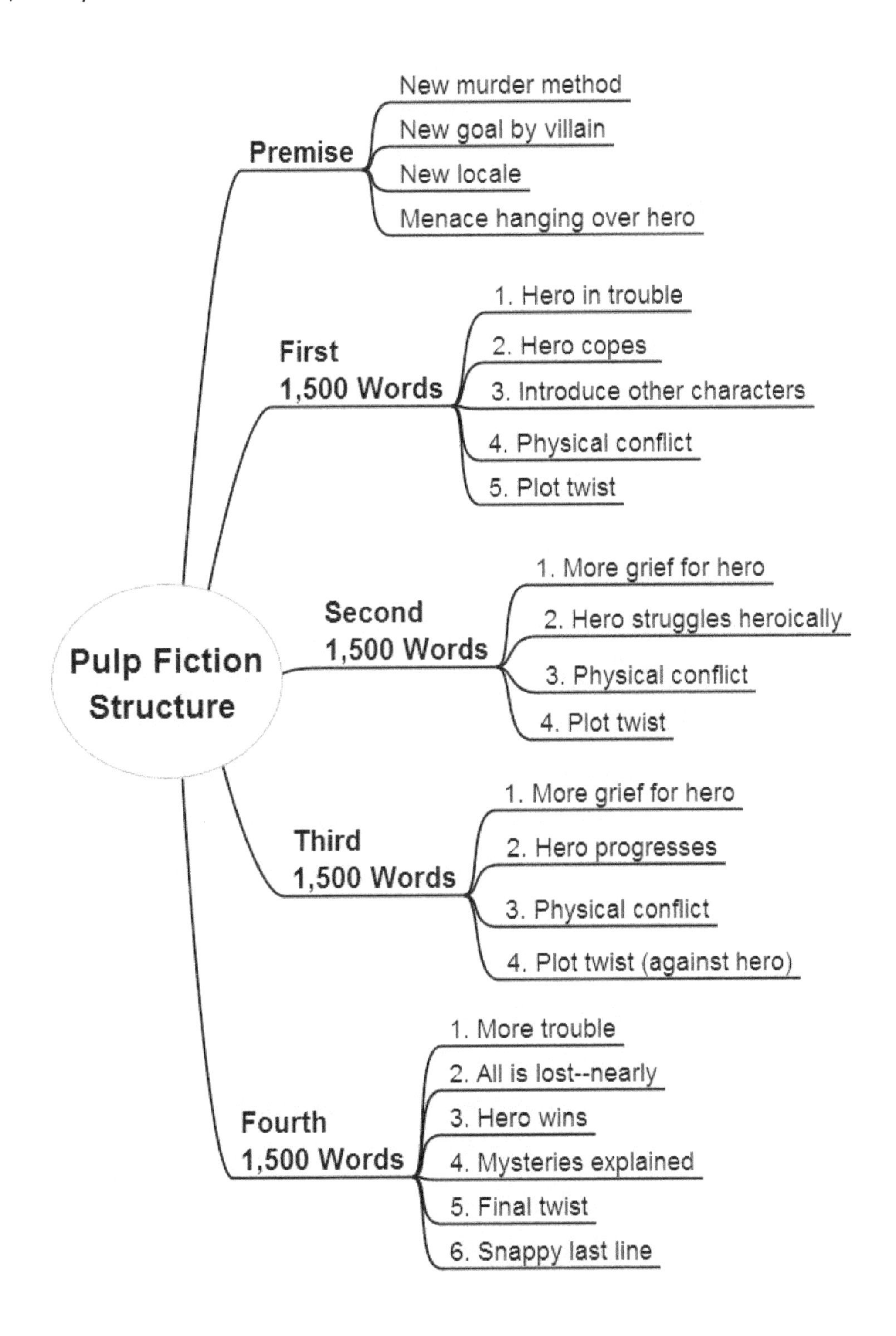

There is no word for what revenge relieves,
because it's never simple what it achieves.
At least, the dead can't harm again,
and righteous avengers can die like other men.

100 Original Story Premises

In logic, a premise is a proposition supporting a conclusion. In fiction, it is the identification of a journey into the unknown. In its simplest form it identifies the protagonist, what he or she needs, and the resolution. I haven't included the resolutions in these conjectured premises but do suggest what knowledge would be needed to write an exceptional story. The citations given are from the movies, TV shows, novels, and short stories that inspired the premises.

1. Investigator who can expand his senses at a crime scene pursues a methodical killer; need a knowledge of extreme sensual abilities
2. Detective uses a variety of drugs and methods of application against suspects; need knowledge of potential "truth serums," including hallucinogenic drugs
3. Musician who wrote a song about a murdered young girl is targeted by the killer; need to write songs
4. Detective uses vivid dreaming to reconstruct the crime scene and review evidence; need knowledge of vivid dreaming
5. Detective with an eidetic memory has periodic amnesia; need knowledge of amnesia—*Unforgettable*
6. Tarot card reader who publically predicted a murder flees while trying to convince the killer she is a phony; need knowledge of tarot cards
7. Detective masters lying as a tool for catching criminals; need to know how to lie convincingly and consistently to a single purpose
8. A street rat who sells information to whoever he thinks will pay the most chooses the wrong client; need to know about street life
9. Small town police chief covers his own killings while facing public outrage; need knowledge of small town police departments—*Banshee*
10. Epileptic girl predicts crimes after convulsions; need knowledge of epilepsy—*Blindspot*
11. FBI director uses subtle and overt ways to protect a militaristic cult; need to know the director's authority and the FBI's resources
12. Murderer leaves a trail of clues on YouTube videos; need a bloody good reason—*Scream*
13. Liberal FBI agents are assassinated by a group of fascists within the bureau; manipulating a presidential election is a good beginning—*Quantico*
14. After his wife is murdered, a judge bribes or threatens every criminal in the search for her killer; need to know a judge's duties and authorities—*Hand of God*
15. A blogger specializing in mind games spars with a murderous opponent; need to know about game blogging—*Eye Candy*

16. Criminal profiler who was publically humiliated goes undercover to gain real-world knowledge of criminals; need knowledge of profiling pitfalls
17. Fake telepath who consults police on the veracity of suspects must catch a serial killer he missed; need to know interrogation methods—*The Listener*
18. Rogue CIA agent gradually kills off a gang of drug and weapons dealers; need to know how international gangs operate
19. Forensic scientist specializes in convictions without a body; need to know a wide range of forensic tools—*Forensic Files*
20. Cursed investigator is murdered and reborn repeatedly until an assassination leading to war is prevented; need imagination only—*Edge of Tomorrow*
21. Artistic psychopath posts storyboards of his crimes on an anime blog; need knowledge of Japanese anime
22. Forensic pathologist finds an increasingly clear trail of evidence on each new victim of a serial killer; need some knowledge of forensic pathology
23. Beautiful, young lesbian seduces, robs, and kills wealthy older women; need knowledge of lesbian killers
24. Billionaire's will forces his children to find his murderer; need to know the laws governing the implementation of a will
25. Man flees his murderous twin while trying to investigate the reason; need to research murders of one twin by the other
26. In the future, a psychiatrist uses induced dream insanity as a tool for blackmail and murder; need to love the unfathomable nature of dreams—*The Little Chinese Dreammaster*[1]
27. Detective uses divination to find his kidnapped lover; need to know how to use the *Yì Jīng*—*A Divination for Her*[2]
28. Model seduces husband and wife detectives into opening a murder cold case; need to know how cold cases are worked
29. LSD user who kills a friend while hallucinating must fabricate an alibi while investigating herself; need to know the effects of LSD in a variety of circumstances—*The Dream Healer*[2]
30. Animal empath uses deadly animals to kill anti-environmentalists; need knowledge of the killing methods of a variety of animals (e.g., venom, suffocation).
31. Two investigators take an empathy drug to defeat a murderous political organization; need a lot of guesses—*The Drug of Choice*[3]
32. Judge who derailed a trial over his belief in the innocence of the accused killer must correct

[1] *The Little Chinese Dreammaster*. Gadfly Books. 2015.

[2] *In*: *Chinese Short Stories*. Gadfly Books. 2015.

[3] *In*: *Crime With My Coffee: Stories, Ballads, Poems, and more with Joe*. Gadfly Books. 2016.

his mistake; need to know how judges can manipulate trials

33. Biochemist who develops a cheap cure for diabetes is hunted by a drug company's assassin; need knowledge of diabetes and drug companies—*The Ignorant Gene*[3]
34. Killer with an eidetic memory experiences repulsion at his first murder but then reconciliation, fascination, pride, and obsession in order; need to magnify each of the stages—*The Memories of Killers*[3] and in "Extras"
35. Homicide detective kills to prove a rival's incompetence but misjudges the self-effacing man; need to know about police rivalries
36. Scarred ex-model divides men who are strongly attracted to her into victims or lovers; need to know the effects of scarring—*Scar*[3]
37. Psychopath whose twin was murdered specializes in kidnapping twins and killing one to study the reactions of the other; need to know the basics of twin biology and psychology—*Almost Identical Twins*[3]
38. Injured detective who convinces the doctors she has amnesia conducts a private investigation; need to know how real amnesiacs behave—*The Blue Gardenia*
39. Murderous twins who can trade personalities to create alibis are pursued by twin brothers who are detectives; see premise 37
40. Killer believes a magical object (e.g., ring, talisman, jewel) protects him from the police; need a wild imagination
41. Woman injured in a burglary wakes with her memories reversed; need knowledge of how memory works—*The Nightingale Floor Murders* [Story 1 below]
42. Using a stolen nootropic, an investigator matches wits with a genius villain; need a fascination for genius—*The Drug of Choice*[3], *The Perverted Genius of Mimi Chen* [Story 3 below]
43. Mother expertly poisons gang members to protect her son; need knowledge of poisons and gang culture
44. FBI cell within a hate group gradually eliminates the leaders; need knowledge of militarized hate groups in the US
45. Superstitious psychopath believes he can steal a victim's luck; need to know many small and large superstitions—*Good Luck Chuck*
46. Story is told through the eyes of the children of the victim, killer, and detective; need to think like a child, not like an ignorant adult—*The Wire*
47. Detective who killed during a drug-induced blackout must investigate himself to discover why; need knowledge of crimes committed during blackouts
48. Medical examiner hides evidence of killings committed by her son; need to know basic

forensics—*Syn*[4]

49. Research student engineers her supervisor's murder; need knowledge of paranoia—*The Perverted Genius of Mimi Chen* [Story 3 below]
50. Arrogance over a specific psychological condition (e.g., synesthesia) leads to torture and murder; need knowledge of the chosen condition—*Canaan, Syn*[4]
51. Hallucinogenic drug helps an investigator prevent a torture and murder; need knowledge of hallucinogenic drugs—*False Syn*[4]
52. Friends swap wives to swap murders; need sex scenes—*Strangers on a Train*
53. Former detective goes undercover to redeem himself for cowardice; need to treat the redemption slowly and carefully—*Four Feathers*
54. The first android detective escapes destruction by human colleagues and seeks revenge; need to create a hostile environment for the android—*Almost Human*
55. Killer experiments with different motives; need to create crimes scenes that match the motive and weapon—*Motive*
56. Geneticist who develops DNA-altering cures for diseases is murdered by an assassin of a medical association; need knowledge of genetic-related diseases
57. Failing detective's attempts to incite crimes he can solve lead to his murder; need to create a variety of sting operations
58. Crime analyst develops a worldwide database of lies told by different kinds of murderers to help her identify murder suspects; need a working classification of lies (e.g., compassionate, utilitarian)
59. Bubonic plague during a heatwave in Texas provides opportunities for murder; need to know about bubonic plague and heatwaves—*The Superior Men of Xinjiang*
60. Detective's secret drawings of the hypothetical perpetrator become increasingly like her partner; need a series of drawings—*Legends*
61. CIA task force must destroy a Chinese lab working on a race-specific virus; need some knowledge of Mandarin and Chinese politics—*The Color of Ice*
62. Two Mandarin-speaking FBI agents track criminals specializing in body parts to Sichuan; need some knowledge of Mandarin, body-part business, and Chinese geography
63. Color-blind detective sees full color during dangerous situations; need to know the advantages and disadvantages of being blind to different colors—*John Doe*
64. Man murders his twin and takes his identity with the help of his brother's wife; see premise 37—*The Postman Always Rings Twice*
65. Beautiful psychiatrist seduces and manipulates patients into committing crimes; need to know methods of seduction—*I, The Jury*

---

[4] *In*: *The Bellingham and Gutierrez Crime Series.* Gadfly Books. 2015.

66. Chief of police in a small western city stages a gangland assassination to improve his chances of being re-elected; need to know small city politics
67. Hideous crime is described similarly by the witnesses, but the investigator believes all are wrong; need to know the reliability of eye witnesses—*Rashomon*
68. Man who dreamed he committed a murder searches for the dream victim to deny or accept the act in reality; need imagination only—*Sliding Doors*
69. Man wrongly accused of murder proves his innocence from a jail cell; need to know about communication between prisons and the outside
70. Woman traps the man who destroyed her husband's career in a rigged house; need knowledge of non-lethal and lethal human traps
71. Unbearable empathy for an abused child forces a stranger to seek vengeance on the perpetrator; need knowledge of the effects of empathy
72. Investigator gradually loses memories of himself as he tracks a killer; need knowledge of the nature of memory loss
73. Eye witness to a murder pretends weakness but is a weapon's expert; need knowledge of many weapons
74. Minority policeman frames a racist detective for a cold case murder the detective worked on; see premise 28
75. Killer struggles against overpowering flashbacks that threaten to expose him; need to create a series of snapshots of the murder in the killer's head
76. Ultra-left cult kills the greediest CEOs to force the business world to become more socialistic; need knowledge of corporate greed
77. CIA agent kills a journalist to prevent being exposed as the whistleblower; need knowledge of the CIA organization—*Berlin Station*
78. Corrupt police station changes after two wives of police officers are murdered; need to know how police stations are organized
79. Educated prostitute investigates the death of her favorite client; need knowledge of elite prostitution
80. Woman detective helps the wife of a murder victim get illegal revenge; need a strong reason (e.g., sex, money, or both)—*The Nightingale Floor Murders* [Story 1 below]
81. Detective who is a "super-recognizer" uses her ability to remember postures and movements to catch a serial killer; need good descriptions of postures and movements
82. Detective believes a blues singer writes songs based on his own crimes; need to write blues songs—*32-20 Blues*
83. Man who went bankrupt because of overpriced medication forces the CEO to ingest dangerous fake medicines; need to know about critical and fake drugs

84. Detective must deduce which literary agents a writer will kill and which methods from rejected novels he will use; need to know how literary agents operate
85. Detective believes a man killed his wife's lover and she killed his in revenge but neither is cooperating; need convincing characterizations of the husband and wife
86. Detective exchanges information with a ghetto gang for targeted killings of other criminals; need to know examples of police and gang cooperation
87. First use of forensic "E-nose" technology that can record all the smells at a crime scene to a fine degree identifies a murder suspect; need to know the abilities of dogs and current scent technology
88. Civil rights activist who specializes in exposing the racial impurities of white supremacists is murdered; need to know basic racial genetics
89. Forensic scientist repeatedly falsifies evidence to increase her success rate; see premise 48—*Trails of Evidence: How Forensic Science Works*
90. Juror is poisoned by one of the other jurors after causing weeks of unnecessary deliberations; need knowledge of the jury system and how jurors behave during long trials
91. Defense lawyer interested in sensationalizing his murder case loses evidence he delayed presenting; need to know the basics of murder defenses
92. Chief witness for the prosecution blackmails the defendant and flees the police and defendant; need to know the basics of murder prosecutions
93. Juror profiler manipulates jury selections for bribes; need to know about jury selection
94. Criminalist becomes obsessed with being the world expert on different methods of murder; need knowledge of a variety of unsolved murders
95. Expert at destroying alibis has the tables turned on her after becoming a suspect in a murder case; need to know how alibi specialists work
96. After fleeing with her children, the hunted wife of a gangster turns hunter with a new lover; need to know how modern gangsters live
97. Juror becomes obsessed with the guilt of a murder suspect she helped free; see premise 90
98. Hounding by police drives an innocent man to murder; need knowledge of police harassment
99. Academic kills a rival in a deluded competition for a Nobel Prize; need knowledge of chemistry, economics, literature, peace, physics, physiology, or medicine and the criteria for winning
100. SWAT officer abandoned by her male colleagues during an intense firefight with a militia hides, plans, and then traps team members one by one; need knowledge of SWAT tactics and human trapping

50 Types of Plot Twists

Presented here are a number of plot twists potentially useful in murder stories (References 1, 2, 3). For more twists and numerous examples from a wide range of genres and literary forms, see Reference 3.

1. **Discovery**: The protagonist or villain discovers his or her true identity or nature.
2. **Flashback:** A vivid description of a past event (1) answers a mystery, (2) expands on a character's personality, or (3) explains the reason for an action.
3. **Unreliable Narrator:** The narration of much of the story is made unreliable to provide the story's premier plot twist at the end.
4. **Reversal:** A sudden but logical reversal in the protagonist's fortunes, for good or ill.
5. **Deus ex Machina:** An unexpected and artificial or improbable device used to resolve an untenable situation or plot.
6. **Poetic Justice:** Virtue is rewarded and/or evil punished, usually in expected but still satisfying ways.
7. **Chekov's Gun:** A character, action, or situation that appears to have little importance in the beginning is revealed as being central to the story later.
8. **Red Herring:** Purposeful misdirection leads the protagonist and readers to the wrong conclusion temporarily or until the true resolution.
9. **In Medias Res:** The story begins in the middle and uses flashbacks to add essential background information before progressing towards the end.
10. **Non-linear Narrative:** The plot is presented in non-chronological order with the time of each segment identified in various ways.
11. **Reverse Chronology:** The consequences are presented before the conflict.
12. **Open Ending:** An ambiguous ending leaves it to the reader to decide what happens to the protagonist, antagonist, or both.
13. **Reversed Roles:** The protagonist and antagonist change roles, usually suddenly and therefore shockingly.
14. **Unexpected Death:** A major character, perhaps even the initial protagonist, unexpectedly dies, usually violently.
15. **Dream Story:** At the end, the story is revealed as a dream or hallucination.
16. **Real Problem:** The inciting incident in the beginning is not the real problem, which is more

severe.

17. **Betrayal:** The protagonist is betrayed by an unlikely character (e.g., spouse, beloved teacher).

18. **Accidental Public Confession:** The antagonist reveals his or her guilt when provoked, overheard, or mistakenly believes the protagonist already knows.

19. **Backstab Backfire:** The antagonist responds to mercy by attempting to kill the protagonist but fails.

20. **Be Careful What You Wish For:** What the protagonist or antagonist wish for turns out to be much less than what they expected.

21. **The Man Behind the Man:** The exposed villain is revealed as a flunkey, puppet, or spokesman for the real villain.

22. **The Reward is a Lie:** The protagonist is promised a reward to do something, but after the deed is done the antagonist reveals the promise to be a lie (and now is free to kill the protagonist).

23. **Career Ending Injury:** An injury to the protagonist or antagonist causes a major shift in the drama (e.g., protagonist must find the killer from a wheel chair).

24. **Daydream Surprise:** A segment of the story that appears to be a continuation of events is revealed to be a daydream fantasy of one of the characters.

25. **Didn't See That Coming:** The protagonist's plan of action fails because of something he or she didn't know existed.

26. **Genuine Impostor:** A character is revealed to be the person he or she is impersonating.

27. **Mask of Sanity:** The antagonist appears normal but is insane.

28. **Revelation:** Information given about a character or situation significantly changes the direction of the story. It is not known beforehand by the characters or readers, and may or may not be a **discovery**.

29. **Secretly Dying:** The protagonist or antagonist is revealed, usually late in the story, to be dying and that accounts for his or her behavior.

30. **Superweapon Surprise:** A character who is initially presented as weak and defenseless is revealed as neither.

31. **Third Option:** When given two options by the antagonist, the protagonist finds a clever third option that temporarily or permanently ends the conflict.

32. **Detail Surprise:** The late appearance of an important detail leads to the story's resolution. This twist differs from a **revelation** in that the characters know it (but consider it

unimportant).

33. **Plot Untwist:** A resolution that appears too obvious is the eventual resolution.
34. **Unexpected Character:** An unexpected character appears in the story, either temporarily or to the end.
35. **Villainous Legacy:** Although dead or imprisoned, the antagonist continues his or her villainy through relatives, disciples, or copycats.
36. **Waking Up Elsewhere:** After an accident, fight, or being drugged, the protagonist wakes up in an unfamiliar place (e.g., prison, hospital) accused of having committed a crime during his or her blackout.
37. **Poetic Injustice:** The villain is never caught because the protagonist is stupid, criminal, or unlucky. This is also an ending.
38. **Reverse Mole:** A character who appears to have evil motives has good ones. The "mole" is a spy version of **Betrayal**.
39. **Faked Death:** A character fakes his or her death and remains hidden until the climax.
40. **Double Agent:** A major character is revealed to be a double agent or someone playing both sides against each other.
41. **Surrender:** The protagonist permits himself or herself to be captured as part of his or her plan for capturing the antagonist.
42. **Unwitting Pawn:** A character eventually realizes he or she has been aiding the villain.
43. **Hopeful Moment:** On the verge of defeat, the protagonist finds a glimmer of hope, either a potential escape or a hidden strength. The hope may be realized or crushed.
44. **Amnesiac Dissonance:** A character recalls a past shockingly different than his or her current life.
45. **Mystery Cult:** The villain belongs to a cult that uses legal and illegal means to thwart the protagonist.
46. **Personal Effects:** After a character dies, a letter, photograph, or object among his or her personal effects reveals the true villain or the motive for the character's actions. This twist can be a story ending.
47. **Motive Reversal:** The villain's initial motive for the conflict unexpectedly changes because he or she wants more violence, fame, or money.
48. **Fake Victory:** The protagonist's initial victory over the antagonist is only apparent.
49. **Destroying Evidence:** A character destroys evidence for any number of reasons (e.g., he or

she is the villain, wants to protect a potential victim, wants to punish the villain personally).

50. **Everybody Did It:** All the major suspects are guilty. This is a twist ending.

References

1. Plot Twist:

   https://en.wikipedia.org/wiki/Plot_twist

2. 25 Turns, Pivots, And Twists To Complicate Your Story:

   http://terribleminds.com/ramble/2013/03/19/25-turns-pivots-and-twists-to-complicate-your-story/

3. Plot Twist:

   http://tvtropes.org/pmwiki/pmwiki.php/Main/PlotTwist

50 Types of Story Endings

Presented here are types of story endings, most from Reference 1, selected for potential relevance to murder stories. Some story endings are also plot twists.

1. **Circular**: The end of the story refers back to the beginning to emphasize a point or close out the story. Also called "Bookends." This is the classic form for research publications. A hypothesis is presented at the beginning and the results favoring and disfavoring the hypothesis are discussed at the end.
2. **Unexpected:** A seemingly improbable ending made to appear logical.
3. **Moral:** The protagonist, antagonist, or both learn a moral lesson.
4. **Emotional:** The ending is satisfying emotionally rather than intellectually.
5. **Question:** Readers are left with a question to increase their involvement in the story and make it more memorable.
6. **Reflective:** The narrator reflects on the meaning of what has happened.
7. **Cliffhanger:** The story ends with no clear resolution.
8. **Multiples:** Several different endings are provided.
9. **Humorous:** The story ends with a humorous conclusion, such as bizarre justice for the protagonist.
10. **Visionary:** The story ends with a vision of a better or worse future.
11. **Dialogue:** The ending consists of a conversation, quote, song, or poem that reveals a moral or more about the protagonist.
12. **Linear:** The story progresses linearly towards a natural resolution.
13. **Open:** It is left to the reader to decide what happens to the protagonist and/or antagonist. This is also a plot twist.
14. **It Was Just a Dream:** The story is revealed at the end to have been a dream or hallucination.
15. **Stinger:** A startling piece of information at the end of the story resolves the conflict.
16. **Adventure Continues:** After the current story's resolution, the protagonist begins another related adventure, which is briefly described.
17. **Anti-climax:** The story builds towards an exciting, uncertain ending but ends sooner or

with less danger to the protagonist than anticipated.

18. **Hero's Reward:** As his or her reward for defeating the villain, the protagonist wins a lover, money, promotion, fame, acceptance, or some other reward.

19. **Bittersweet:** The defeat of the villain comes at the cost of lives, love, honor, or something else of great value to the protagonist.

20. **Bluffing the Murderer:** When the protagonist doesn't have enough evidence for a conviction, he or she tricks the villain into exposing more evidence by lying, forging evidence, or scaring the villain.

21. **Fatigue:** The story continues past the expected ending.

22. **Leaving:** After the resolution, the protagonist travels for a vaguely identified reason (e.g., call of the open road; continuing an unidentified search).

23. **Simple Life**: The protagonist gives up fighting crime to become a farmer, fisherman, musician, etc. as a reaction to the ugliness he or she had faced. Also named "Call to Agriculture."

24. **Broadcast**: The villain appears to have won, but an incriminating document or video, possibly after the protagonist has been killed, exposes him or her.

25. **Shootout**: The good guy and bad guy shoot it out at the end, often in a darkened building with the good guy killing the bad guy with his last bullet.

26. **Dénouement**: After the climax, the remaining mysteries are explained and the fates of the characters identified.

27. **Destroying Evidence:** A character unexpectedly destroys significant evidence of a crime for one of many reasons (e.g., he or she is the villain, wants to protect the victim, wants to punish the villain personally).

28. **Deus ex Machina:** An artificial or improbable device is used to resolve an untenable situation or plot. In other words, they are unexpected, implausible, and external solutions that aid the protagonist.

29. **Diabolus ex Machina:** This is the opposite of deus ex machina: The introduction of a character or event that makes the protagonist's situation suddenly worse. This trope is usually reserved for the endings of stories in a series.

30. **Distant Finale:** An account of the main characters is presented some time, usually years, after the resolution of the story's conflict.

31. **The Dog Bites Back:** A long-suffering victim of manipulation, bullying, or abuse gets revenge. This may be the end or the beginning of the end for the villain.

32. **Doomed Protagonist:** The protagonist faces an inevitable death but continues to seek

revenge or justice.

33. **Door Closing:** In TV shows and film more than books, the last scene is a door closing, either to leave the audience guessing what will happen next or as symbolic closure.

34. **Hero Sacrifice:** A main character, usually the protagonist but sometimes the villain, sacrifices himself or herself to save a loved one or someone innocent.

35. **Bad Guy Wins:** Although the villain wins, the victory is rarely portrayed as complete unless a sequel is intended.

36. **Memorial Service:** The story ends with a real or sham funeral of a significant character.

37. **Epilogue Letter:** The remaining mysteries and consequences are explained in a letter to or from the protagonist.

38. **Everybody Did It:** All the major suspects are guilty. This is also a plot twist.

39. **Team Disbanded:** After a successful investigation, the investigation team (invariably of unusual composition) is disbanded, though with a hint they may get back together for special cases.

40. **Foregone Conclusion:** The murderer is identified at the beginning, and the remaining story is about why the murder was committed.

41. **Happily Ever After:** Self-explanatory. This ending is rarely suitable for stories in which the protagonist is a professional investigator because he or she has more murders to solve and too much baggage.

42. **Accidental Public Confession:** The antagonist reveals his or her guilt when provoked, overheard, or mistakenly believes the protagonist already knows.

43. **Framing the Guilty:** The protagonist is forced to frame the villain because enough concrete evidence doesn't exist.

44. **Sympathy for the Devil:** The protagonist shows some sympathy for the cause or suffering of the villain while believing that legal justice must be served.

45. **Third Option:** When given two options by the antagonist, the protagonist finds a clever third option that ends the conflict.

46. **Exit, Pursued by a Bear:** Moral but not legal justice is achieved by someone other than the protagonist. The protagonist may voluntarily or involuntarily give up the villain to the avenger.

47. **Forced Consent:** The protagonist is forced to accept the corruption of superiors to take down a bigger villain or save a potential victim (and possibly to avoid dismissal, imprisonment, or death).

48. **Villainous Victim:** The victim is ultimately revealed as deserving death. The killer may or may not be let go by the protagonist.

49. **Burning the Past:** The protagonist burns photographs or documents to symbolize a complete break with his or her past. Alternatively, he or she may throw some valued object (e.g., badge, award, ring) away.

50. **We'll Meet Again:** This vow may be utter by the villain as he or she is being taken to prison or by the protagonist as the villain escapes.

Reference

1. Ending Tropes:

   http://tvtropes.org/pmwiki/pmwiki.php/Main/EndingTropes

Sample Plotlines

Note: When reviewing the sample plotlines, keep in mind the selected facets and their sequence depend on both the premise and the story's structure not on the order of the maps. For example, to make the story a mystery, the who, how, why, or all three must be hidden until the end. As you prepare your own plotlines by going through the 19 facets repeatedly, the order should become clearer as details that fit the premise are added. Like the facets, the initial details can be kept or replaced as the plotline evolves.

A Game of Terror

On one side are a hundred good guys.
On the other side are a hundred bad guys.
All have AK47s.

Now send the good guys against the bad guys
after
removing the good guys who are
frightened,
untrained,
selfish,
weak,
afraid of hurting innocents,
and
incapable of killing another human.

Alas, this game is like ill-fated reality
in that
the bad guys are none or few of these things
and
they get to shoot first.

Your chance of winning is very, very small,
and if the bad guys are willing to die,
almost none at all.

Plotlines of the Sample Stories

Here are the evolved plotlines of the three short stories given below. In all three, a woman commits murder but gets revenge (disguised as self-defense) in the first, is caught in the second, and escapes in the third. They are written in a minimalistic style.

Plot 1

This plotline is based on the premise of the first story (*The Nightingale Floor Murders*): *A young woman whose memory has regressed must search for what seem to be very old clues to her husband's murder and the attack that caused her unique condition.* It has a tinge of fantasy as well as a heavy dose of crime. The plot structure is linear with a character twist at the end.

1. **Protagonist:** Citizen Jane, a young woman who escapes from the killer of her husband; personal interest; vigilante attitude.
2. **Killer:** Single murderer; kills once; sane (but drugged); kills neighbor during a night-time robbery; protagonist escapes.
3. **Accomplice:** None.
4. **Victim:** Wealthy neighbor of the killer. Protagonist shot while escaping; had a brief, regretted affair with the killer.
5. **Motive:** Both impersonal and personal; greed with depraved indifference and revenge on the protagonist.
6. **Plan:** Premeditated, with risk assessment. Killer intends forcing the owners to open their home safe and killing them. Motivator: Drug induced arrogance. Subsequent reaction: Anger and anxiety over protagonist's escape; he must kill her before she recovers her memory of that night.
7. **Site:** Planned, with positive risk assessment; mansion in New Haven. Environment uniquely unfavorable (nightingale floors), but worth risking. Killer intends leaving the bodies.
8. **Action**: Active and cold-blooded after being unexpectedly confronted by armed owner. Victim shot when he hesitates. Protagonist leaves by an emergency ladder after hearing her husband call the neighbor's name. Later, protagonist traps the killer with the help of the woman detective on the case. The two women are lovers.
9. **Weapon:** Active: 9 mm pistol for killer; .45 pistol for protagonist.
10. **Injury:** Killer not injured; husband dead; protagonist shot in head.
11. **Cover-up:** None before killing. At murder scene, killer wears gloves. After murder, killer leaves husband's body and looks for the protagonist.
12. **Alibi:** None, from drugged arrogance and living nearby. Fears being caught until the protagonist is dead.
13. **Detection:** Two detectives closing in on the killer. Protagonist begins extensive memory

rehabilitation.

14. **Witness:** Potentially the protagonist.
15. **Evidence:** Only evidence is a single word that may or may not be in the protagonist's retrievable memory. No useful forensics.
16. **Arrest:** None.
17. **Trial:** None. Protagonist murders antagonist but her action is legally judged self-defense.
18. **Sentence:** None.
19. **Justice:** Moral justice served.

* * *

Plot 2

This plotline is based on the premise of the second story (*From Tulips to Emeralds*): *An American student and a young Moroccan boy are murdered near each other on the same night in Utrecht.* The plot structure is linear with a partial cliffhanger ending.

1. **Protagonist:** Dutch Inspector of police, whose interest is professional; young Dutch woman, whose interest is personal; two New Haven detectives, whose interests are professional.
2. **Killer:** Single murderer commits two murders. Sanity questionable.
3. **Accomplice:** Colleague of the American victim.
4. **Victim:** American student visiting Utrecht killed for personal reasons. Local Moroccan boy killed for an impersonal reason.
5. **Motive:** Personal for the American victim; anger and jealousy over rejection as a lover and as a co-author on a significant academic publication. Impersonal for Moroccan boy; killed for being a witness.
6. **Plan:** Premeditated: Killing of American with some risk assessment; motivator is revenge; subsequent reaction is anxiety. Opportunistic: Killing of Moroccan boy; motivator is personal safety; subsequent reaction is indifference.
7. **Site:** Planned, with some risk assessment. Environment favors killer. Leaves American in the street; puts small Moroccan in a dumpster.
8. **Action**: Active. American's throat cut while cycling; Morocaan's throat cut while fleeing drunk and stoned. First killing is a crime of passion; second killing is a cover-up.
9. **Weapon:** Long-bladed knife.
10. **Injury:** None to killer. Both victims die before being found.
11. **Cover-up:** Before: Travels to Europe for a conference. During: Wears gloves and a motorcycle helmet; purchases weapon in Brussels; kills witness. After: Dumps knife far from the crime scene. Couldn't move the large American; puts Moroccan boy in dumpster to gain time to return to Brussels.

12. **Alibi:** Attending an academic conference in Brussels. Believes the death of the Moroccan will confuse the crime.
13. **Detection:** Dutch leads dry up. Dutch detective and American's Dutch girlfriend go to New Haven. Girlfriend identifies suspects. Dutch and New Haven detectives expose killer. New Haven forensic team finds incriminating evidence.
14. **Witness:** Only witness is the murdered Moroccan boy.
15. **Evidence:** History of conflict between killer (supervisor and ex-lover) and student; trace of Moroccan boy's blood on killer's motorcycle helmet; similarity of throat cuts.
16. **Arrest:** Killer arrested in New Haven. Eventually extradited to The Netherlands.
17. **Trial:** In the future.
18. **Sentencing:** In the future.
19. **Justice:** Partial legal and moral justice served. Accomplice remains free, but evidence of his involvement may still be found.

* * *

Plot 3

This plotline is based on the premise of the third story (*The Perverted Genius of Mimi Chen*): *A brilliant young graduate student engineers the murder of her supervisor and the successful swindle of the Chinese government over a nootropic drug.* Like the first story, this one has a tinge of fantasy. The plot alternates between the investigation and Chen's activities, and while the two lines are linear they are not synchronous. The ending is a cliffhanger.

1. **Protagonist:** A young Ph.D. student (Mimi Chen) in biochemistry. She is interested in crime as a professional tool.
2. **Killer:** Chen masterminds two murders and one suicide and kills two kidnappers in self-defense. Possibly insane but highly focused and methodical.
3. **Accomplice:** Chinese Ambassador to the United States, military attaché, and martial arts master. All involuntary.
4. **Victim:** Professor of biochemistry unknown to assassin (martial artist) but known to Chen. Assassin commits suicide. Ambassador's death is also instigated by Chen. She wounds the military attaché and kills two Chinese soldiers. None of the deaths are personal.
5. **Motive:** Impersonal: Potential for great fame and immense wealth. Career goal unknown.
6. **Plan:** Carefully premeditated murders with meticulous risk assessment. Motivator is arrogance with a specific, unidentified goal. Subsequent reaction to all four deaths is indifference except as they relate to her goal.
7. **Site:** Planned by Chen: Murder of professor in his lab. Unplanned by Chen: Location of assassin's suicide and of the Ambassador's elimination by the Chinese Central Military Commission (CMC). Also unplanned by Chen (but prepared): Wounding of military attaché and killing of soldiers during a meeting in a park.

8. **Action**: Active and passive. Professor and soldiers killed with small caliber bullets from different guns. Assassin cuts his own throat. Ambassador killed by CMC by unknown method. Professor's laptop stolen by the killer.
9. **Weapon:** Active: Two small caliber pistols; butterfly knife. Unknown for the Ambassador.
10. **Injury:** None to killer of the professor, though he eventually commits suicide. None to Chen or CMC. Among Chen's enemies, five are dead and one is wounded.
11. **Cover-up:** Chen uses other people or kills in self-defense.
12. **Alibi:** Same as cover-up.
13. **Detection:** None. A retired professor and three detectives believe Chen had her supervisor murdered, but have no evidence. They don't know about the deaths of the Ambassador or soldiers.
14. **Witness:** Retired professor is the most dangerous potential witness. Chen isn't worried.
15. **Evidence:** None. Chen is only a suspect because she benefits the most from the professor's death.
16. **Arrest:** None.
17. **Trial:** None.
18. **Sentence:** None.
19. **Justice:** Only from Chen's view.

* * *

First she estimated the time between the first shot, the one that killed Mr. Clayden, and the second shot, the one that wounded Mrs. Clayden. She also estimated the time Mrs. Clayden needed to go from behind the bedroom door to the spot on the lawn where she had been shot. For the first estimate, she had her partner dash from the lowest step the shooter could have been to the balcony rail, allowing several seconds for bashing in the bedroom door. For the second, she timed herself rushing to the balcony, swinging over the rail, scurrying down the ladder, and running to the marked spot.

"Detective, haven't you heard the expression, 'academia is a den of vipers'? The seriousness of this business would make a gangster blush. *For example*, the fewer the names on a scientific publication in a top journal, the better for those named. Understand?"

The Nightingale Floor Murders

The man woke his wife. "Adaline," he whispered, "we have an intruder. Be very quiet."

As she woke, her sleepy face turned fearful. When the dim light from the backyard security lamps revealed her husband removing the pistol from the nightstand, fear turned to fright. "Caleb. Call the police."

He turned and knelt in front of her. "Our cellphones are in the library where we left them during the party and the house line must be cut. I'll wait in the hall near the top of the stairs. Here's what I want you to do. Lock the bedroom door quietly, put on a jacket and your running shoes, open the balcony door, and play out the emergency ladder. If I yell or you hear shots, climb down the ladder and run, not to the street because the intruder may have friends waiting. Go to the back fence and through the forest." It was the beginning of her jogging track and she would be able to navigate it at night faster than any intruder.

"What happened to the alarm system?"

"I'll give the company hell in the morning. I'm going. Do what we planned." He kissed her forehead as he rose.

Caleb had subconsciously recognized the barely audible squeals, creaks, and chirps of the wooden floor in the main hallway. They were from the "nightingale floor," the eccentricity he had presented that evening to patrons of the annual Clayden Thanksgiving Charity Party. Seven years ago, he began introducing novelties to attract patrons and to, he liked to say, make loosening their purse strings less painful. Adaline loved it and vowed to create a song incorporating the floors many sounds for use as one of her attractions.

The bedroom door was open, and Caleb signaled to his wife to lock it. He slipped out into the hall next to the stairs. He was carrying a customized 1911 Colt .45 pistol, an inheritance from his father. He had never shot this or any other weapon, and it felt huge, heavy, and awkward. Worried about the kick, he put both hands on the gun like he had seen in movies. Caleb learned having no option to run did not automatically create bravery. He was scared.

From the dim, wintery light coming from the third floor skylight, Caleb could see a small way down the spiraling staircase, which had also been one of his Charity novelties. Because sounds of a noisy floor were now prominent in his home, he remembered the Da Vinci staircase also creaked, though in few places. He tried quieting himself with the thought of putting a "stumble step" on the staircase.

Caleb raised the pistol to point down the visible section. He prayed the first sound would come from far below.

At the first creak, he panicked and turned on the chandelier hanging from the third floor ceiling above the stairs. If the intruder was out-of-sight because of the staircase's design, he or she might run away, which was fine with him. Standing on a step within Caleb's sight was a bare-faced, well-dressed, middle-aged man. Caleb had visualized home invaders as young men in street clothes wearing ski masks. This was no thug.

"*John!* What are you doing? Why are you still here?" John Rowley was one of the neighbors who had attended the charity party. On recognizing his friend, Caleb lowered the Colt in relief.

John was caught off-guard by the sudden light and the appearance of Caleb. He was also holding a pistol, a Glock 19 Gen 4. It was a small black gun Caleb didn't see against John's side.

When John didn't answer, Caleb assumed the man was drunk, but he was wrong. During the party, John had stepped outside to smoke a joint soaked in crystal meth. The meth was as easy to get as marijuana. Together they gave John the focus and the callousness he wanted.

When guests had begun leaving, John entered the cloak room with two couples and collected his overcoat, which contained the small Glock. He lingered behind the couples as they walked towards the front door. Instead of leaving, he made his way along a side hallway to the cellar door. In the cellar, he waited. When he believed Caleb and Adaline had gone to bed, he cut the home phone line and disconnected the internet service. He didn't risk disarming the security system because it would trigger an alarm. It would activate when he left the house, but that didn't matter because safety was nearby.

Over the years since meeting Caleb, John had seen his old family money diminish, while Caleb's old money grew. This was Caleb's fault, he liked to think though he knew it wasn't true. The Claydens were exceedingly wealthy and John wanted to be in that class. At the very least, their safe would hold Adaline's extraordinary jewelry.

There was also a tinge of revenge. "I should rape her," he thought as he waited. He wouldn't. Adaline and John had had a brief affair, as brief as possible, one encounter when she was high on marijuana and Caleb was away. Adaline never let John be alone with her again.

"Caleb, my friend," he said in a friendly voice, though he was angry at seeing Caleb with a gun. It was too dangerous dealing with someone with such an easy weapon to use. Adaline would know the combination.

He raised the Glock 19 and shot Caleb. The bullet dug into the man's chest and stayed there. The bullet's rifling would be intact but he had no intention of recovering the slug. It was a matter of time not of revulsion or shame.

Caleb died as he fell backwards, his body landing on the hallway floor and his head against a wall. John climbed the twisting stairs as quickly as possible and ran towards the master bedroom. He could tell which door by the expanse of wall without doors. Guessing it was locked, he kicked the handle with a straight kick next to the knob. The main room was empty. He was prepared to search the bathroom and walk-in closets until he saw the open balcony door. He rushed to the balcony rail.

Adaline hadn't waited for a yell or shot. As soon as she heard her husband call "John," she fled. On the same night she had sex with John, she learned of his drug habit; and she saw an unattractive side of him when she refused to smoke crystal meth with him. She was nearly down the ladder when she heard the shot. It paralyzed her and forced her to look up in the hope of seeing Caleb leaning over the rail. Within seconds, she realized the danger and dropped to the ground, turned, and ran.

Adaline didn't hear the second shot. She was hit and blacked out. When she woke, she clawed the lawn and pushed herself to her feet. She ran towards the back fence. Without conscious thought, she found the key, unlocked the gate, and ran into the forest. After a few steps, she believed she was going for a jog.

Because Adaline had fallen hard and didn't move on the ground, John assumed she was dead. He turned away in anger because now he had no way of opening the safe and the gunshot would bring the police. His hope was Caleb hadn't put the necklace Adaline had worn that night in the safe. Seeing it had made him ecstatic. Because a drunken Caleb may have left the safe open, John had searched the library before coming upstairs. He found the necklace on Adaline's vanity desk. His elation was short-lived when he remembered how exquisite she had looked that night. The necklace had been her novel presentation. It was a rare "pigeon-blood" ruby, one with a purple hue. In its simple gold setting laying in the cleavage of her white breasts, the jewel had been a greater hit than the nightingale floor with all the men and many of the women.

Perhaps she was still alive, alive enough to tell him the combination. Whether she could or not, he had to make sure she was dead. Having heard Caleb call his name must have been the reason for her trying to escape so early.

Looking over the balcony rail, he saw she was gone. He ran out of the room, down the frustratingly slow staircase, and out of the house to the back yard. The back gate was self-locking and Adaline had taken the key. With no time to climb over the spiked metal gate, he blasted the lock with one shot. Because the police would be there soon and would be checking on neighbors, he had only minutes. If she was as severely wounded as the blood trail suggested, he had a good chance of catching her. The safe wouldn't be opened or moved for days, possibly weeks. If she was not severely wounded, he had little chance because she was so fit.

* * *

After John's second shot, the emergency service received several calls. After the third, more were made to the home of the Chief of Police. The dispatcher also received an alert from the security company. Two patrol cars arrived within ten minutes but were delayed by having to batter open first the front gate and then the front door with a portable ram. It was some time before they found the dead man on the third floor of the mansion.

One of the patrolmen called headquarters and was connected to the Chief. The Chief had already ordered Detectives Katherine Gutierrez and Joseph Bellingham to investigate. He knew from experience moneyed people got a heavy response to blue-collar crime or got angry. The patrolmen were ordered to continue their search but to be careful what they touched. Neither order was necessary. The men knew murders by home invaders meant the whole family, and they had all heard embarrassing accounts of fingerprints being found where they shouldn't have been found.

Gutierrez and Bellingham arrived at 4:18 on a cold, late November morning. New Haven got slightly over two feet of snow a year and had begun working timidly towards the average an hour earlier. The four patrolmen reported finding no other occupants dead or alive and having touched several door handles. They marked the doors.

Inside, the detectives were immediately curious about the nightingale floor and wondered if they reflected an established fear by the Claydens. It was a possible lead. One of the patrolmen led them directly to the body. He showed them the emergency ladder hanging over the balcony rail in the master bedroom. When Bellingham looked into the backyard, he saw two sets of prints in the snow. "The wife may be out there, Katherine. Get your camera because those tracks will be covered soon." The crime scene team was still gathering at police headquarters on Union Avenue.

Gutierrez photographed the clearest sets of footprints and what appeared to be blood splatter. She was tempted to blow off the thin layer of snow but would have had to step closer. She photographed the back gate lock. When she opened the gate, she heard Joe returning. He was walking off the path to avoid destroying evidence. Very little snow had reached the forest floor, and Bellingham had given up when the path ended at a paved road.

Inside the home again, they saw evidence of the charity party in the kitchen but nothing appeared unusual. In the library, they found a hinged bookshelf opened but the safe behind it closed. In the cellar, Bellingham discovered the phone line had been cut and cable/internet disconnected but the security system working.

Within an hour, Gutierrez was on the phone to Chief Tunbridge. She summarized her notes.

Caleb Carlton Clayden, a forty-two year old white male of unknown occupation was found dead at 3:48 on 29th November in his home on Conrad Drive, Westville District. Patrolmen Sanchez, Lacey, Weissmuller, and Lee responded to 911 calls about shots being fired in or near the Clayden residence, and the security company's alert identified the exact location. The bullet is recoverable.

No other occupants, dead or alive, are in the home. In the backyard, there is evidence of a woman, presumably his wife, Adaline Grace Clayden, being wounded and chased by a single man, presumably the killer of her husband. Joe followed the trail into the woods behind the house but lost it.

Motive is unknown. The initial appearance is of a burglary gone bad. Three facts suggest the killer had been familiar with the Claydens: The disguised cover of the safe was open, the phone and internet were disabled in the cellar, and the security system was working. The murderer may have attended a party at the home last night.

When Gutierrez finished, Bellingham told her the dispatcher had notified him of a woman with a head wound being admitted to the Yale-New Haven Hospital. The woman had been found in the Westville District and was white, about forty years old, and blonde. She was unconscious and had no identification. Since the woman was likely to be the victim's wife, Gutierrez collected Mrs. Clayden's purse and some casual clothes. She had also been a traumatized patient.

After waiting several hours at the hospital, Gutierrez and Bellingham met Dr. Maria Ali, the resident surgeon who had operated on Mrs. Clayden. Before taking the detectives to the recovery room, she talked with them in her office. "The Jane Doe had a bullet wound to the back of her head, which is why I notified your department."

"Is she out of danger?" Gutierrez asked.

"The most I can say is she has a good chance. The bullet did less damage than it could have. I'm familiar with the damage a bullet this size can do at close range, and my guess is she was either some distance from the shooter or the cartridge had a subpar load."

Gutierrez said, "She was shot from a third floor balcony at a distance of at least sixty yards. Forensics will provide a more exact distance later."

"I weighed the bullet after removing it. It's a standard 115 grain slug." Dr. Ali handed Gutierrez an envelope with the bullet. An unusual amount of information about Mrs. Clayden's wound was handwritten on a note inside. "It's my specialty, though not by choice. I also keep statistics on the physical conditions of victims and she is one of the fittest I have treated. That means she has good blood flow to the brain."

"And the prognosis?"

"When admitted, she couldn't open her eyes or speak in response to voice commands but could respond to pain. On the standard coma scale, she has severe trauma and could be in a coma for a long time."

"And when she wakes, assuming she does?"

"Impossible to say. Wounds to the brain can result in severe memory loss, confusion, or distorted thinking. Her excellent fitness may make the difference."

"Her name is Adaline Grace Clayden. We'll leave her basic information with the admitting nurse. Her husband was murdered in their home a few hours ago, and she was shot while escaping."

"How awful. She may suffer from psychological trauma even if she recovers all her motor and mental functions."

Bellingham said, "She may also suffer a further attempt on her life so an officer will be stationed by her door. We'll need a list of doctors, nurses, and orderlies who have valid reasons for entering her room. No one alleging to be a family member, friend, or visitor will be permitted for now."

While waiting for a guard, the detectives watched the heavily bandaged, comatose victim and doubted she would ever be able to help them. Their doubts didn't reflect callousness but practical concern. Her future was in God's and the doctor's hands.

* * *

During the month Mrs. Clayden was in a coma, the detectives finished their initial interviews with family, friends, neighbors, and the eighty party guests and reviewed the evidence.

- Mrs. Clayden's clothes had no gunpowder residue.
- The blood on her clothes and the lawn was hers.

- Mrs. Clayden had not said anything coherent to the two joggers who found her semi-conscious along a forest trail.
- The gun found beside Mr. Clayden had not been fired recently.
- Mr. Clayden was killed and Mrs. Clayden wounded with 9 mm, 115 grain bullets from the same gun. No match was found in the Integrated Ballistics Information System (IBIS).
- One set of footprints in the backyard was made by her shoes.
- One set of footprints was made by a man's treadless, probably dress, shoes, size 11.
- The spacing of both sets of footprints indicated the woman and man had been running.
- No fingerprints were found in the home with matches in the Integrated Automated Fingerprint Identification System (IAFIS).
- The nine employees of the catering company testified in oral and written statements they had all left at the same time. None had criminal records.
- The multi-million dollar necklace Mrs. Clayden wore at the party was not found in the master bedroom or in the safe (which was opened by the family's lawyer).
- Interviews with friends and neighbors revealed no affairs by the husband or wife.
- Interviews with party guests produced no obvious leads.
- Evidence suggesting the perpetrator was a guest at the Thanksgiving Party included:
    - The security system working throughout the night.
    - The disguised safe cover being open.
    - The phone and internet being disabled in the cellar.
    - Mrs. Clayden's necklace being stolen on the night she first wore it.

There was an additional piece of evidence pointing to a member of New Haven's high society being the murderer. When Bellingham wondered how Mrs. Clayden had time to get as far as she did, his partner tried answering the question with an experiment. First she estimated the time between the first shot, the one that killed Mr. Clayden, and the second shot, the one that wounded Mrs. Clayden. She also estimated the time Mrs. Clayden needed to go from behind the bedroom door to the spot on the lawn where she had been shot. For the first estimate, she had her partner dash from the lowest step the shooter could have been to the balcony rail, allowing several seconds for bashing in the bedroom door. For the second, she timed herself rushing to the balcony, swinging over the rail, scurrying down the ladder, and running to the marked spot.

"Mrs. Clayden's time is three times longer than the killer's time," she told Bellingham. They were sitting on the bed in the Clayden's master bedroom.

"So she left as soon as Clayden heard the intruder. He may have forced her if he thought the perp was near."

"Perhaps, but it is also possible she recognized the intruder's voice or her husband calling a name."

"In any case, both the evidence and lack of evidence suggest the perpetrator was no street thug."

"We need to investigate the finances of everyone who attended the party."

* * *

The next week, the detectives met with Dr. Ali. The doctor appeared and sounded excited. "When Mrs. Clayden first woke from her coma, I was amazed to see a forty-two year old woman acting and speaking like a five year old child. No actress could have come close."

"Have you seen this before?" Bellingham asked.

"Wait. There is more. Today she is about twelve in behavior and vocabulary, and if the total regression is not unique, the change must be. I am recording everything with her mother's permission."

"You will write about her condition?"

"Certainly. Regression is a mechanism for coping with stress, but that kind is the thumb-sucking kind, small acts. With her physical damage and psychological trauma, the regression is complete, though clearly not permanent, and the change is in the right direction. For me, the greatest mystery here is what is driving the maturity."

Gutierrez asked, "But she is maturing rapidly?"

"Yes, but not enough yet. Come see."

The detectives and Dr. Ali entered a standard two-person hospital room that had been converted at Mrs. Durand's expense into a bedroom. A large screen TV had replaced the small high-mounted hospital TV, and scattered about were toys and games, some from her childhood. Her mother had given her a digital picture frame that displayed photos of Mrs. Clayden from childhood to recently. It lay face down on the floor.

Mrs. Durand was sitting in a corner chair silently watching her daughter. She looked tired and miserable. When she saw Dr. Ali and the detectives, she joined them. She had met the detectives before.

"Adaline still refuses to believe I'm her mother, but at least the screaming to be let go has stopped. I feel like a kidnapper of my own child. And she must feel like a kidnapping victim with no parents and no one helping her escape. I'm taking her home tomorrow, though god knows what she'll do to my lovely home."

"Do you have a piano?" Dr. Ali asked.

"Yes, and she started lessons at five. Thank you, doctor. I rarely had to remind her to practice, and she may feel that way again when we get home."

Gutierrez spoke. "May I suggest something? Games. Athletic games, like tennis, basketball, ping-pong; and equipment. She was exceedingly fit before being shot."

"Yes, Detective Gutierrez. She needs things to explore. Exercise equipment."

"Piano, painting, and..."

Bellingham interrupted, "Martial arts, specifically *taiji* if you can find a teacher. It's a form of meditation in movement that may help calm her mind as well as strengthen her body."

Mrs. Durand thanked the doctor and detectives for the hope they had given her. She left.

While they had talked at the far end of the room from Adaline, they had watched her and she had occasionally looked at them. She was lying on the bed listening to something on a phone, apparently music from her humming. To them, she looked like a relaxed adult.

To Adaline, the doctor had become a snooping guard, someone asking questions gently but still keeping her imprisoned. The detectives were too poorly dressed to be anything but police. After failing with her guards, she knew these police wouldn't help her either. She also knew she would get none from the old woman who kept lying about being her mother. What Adaline couldn't understand was why the woman would buy her almost anything and why she kept coming back.

Adaline stayed still until the doctor and detectives left.

* * *

The Durand estate was in the countryside not far from Boston. Instead of hiding her daughter away, as the New Haven detectives advised, Mrs. Durand added guards and dogs to the estate's electronic security. As Adaline's regression receded, the estate became a prison for her. The cure she discovered made her captivity worse. Psychotherapy, hypnotism, visualization, and other therapies failed. Only exercise, jogging and martial arts, and music, piano playing, gave her relief. For exercise, she focused on movement and pain; for music, she focused on movement and sound. The balance between hours of freedom from confused memories and hours of viewing physical records of the past restored order in her mind. The restoration was gradual but fast enough for her to feel it. That feeling drove her hard.

For martial arts and music, teachers came for private lessons. For jogging, Adaline ran around the grounds until she couldn't stand it anymore. At dawn on a day in July, eight months after being shot, Adaline left the estate. She would have two hours of freedom and open road before her mother woke. "I could go back later, or not at all," she told herself while starting off. She chose to face her mother sooner than later. From that day on, morning runs became a routine. By September, she was spending every morning off the estate, jogging, visiting neighbors, and eating at a country restaurant. It was dangerous freedom, her mother reminded her every day.

At dawn on a mid-September morning, Adaline left with the security guard who followed her in a car as far as he could and met her later at the restaurant. After a mile down the road, Adaline turned on to a forest track. The guard watched until she disappeared and headed to the restaurant.

That morning he waited longer than usual. When he tried phoning her, he got no connection. He was unsure what to do for several minutes. If her phone battery was dead, she would be annoyed if he wasn't there. But if she was hurt...

He sped back towards the beginning of her jogging track and was relieved to see her standing beside the road. When he got closer, he was shocked to see blood on her T-shirt and to see her holding her left arm as if it were broken. He rushed to help her into the car but she refused. "Frank, cut off my shirt. I can't bear it but can't raise my left arm." A combat knife was among his weapons. While Frank cut, she told him, "It's his blood," and gestured vaguely down the track.

Frank called 911 and asked for an ambulance as well as the police. As they waited in the car, she told Frank what had happened. She wasn't sure why, perhaps because he had been a soldier.

Two men had trapped her along a section of the trail with brush and fences on either side. They didn't have guns because they didn't believe they needed them, and because they intended raping her before killing her. She had no doubt about either intention.

The men were a dozen yards in front and a dozen behind when she stopped. Three "laws" from martial arts saved her life: Always use a weapon when possible; almost anything can be a weapon; and attack the most dangerous opponent first. As the men advanced, Adaline searched the ground as fast as she could. Some stretches of the trail were more stony than others, but here the stones were small. She remembered her phone, which was strapped to her upper left arm. She quickly put the phone in her right hand with the front facing outward and ran at the biggest man. The would-be assassin was amused the woman thought she could get past him. By the time he realized she was coming straight for him, he barely had time to raise his arm to strike her down. She ran into him. As he struck downwards, she blocked his right forearm with her left forearm and smashed him straight in the face with the phone. Her hit had the force of her punching arm and the force of her forward movement. Although her block absorbed the man's blow, the impact broke her forearm.

As the man fell backwards, Adaline barely maintained her balance. She spun counterclockwise to her right and threw the phone at the man approaching rapidly behind her. He slowed long enough for her to escape. She ran fast and in great pain back towards the road. After several hundred yards, she risked a look back. The men were gone.

The encounter lasted less than half a minute. When she stopped at the intersection, she was shaking badly but was calmer by the time Frank arrived.

"I was lucky."

Frank shook his head. "No, you used your training." He had been in Iraq and hated the concept of luck. If it wasn't you or your team saving your life, it was simply an escape.

* * *

On the day before Gutierrez heard about the attack, she received an email from Mrs. Clayden. They had corresponded by phone and email many times during the past nine months. Their conversations were first about the case and Mrs. Clayden's progress but gradually became personal. The two women were about the same age, and their friendship was sealed when Gutierrez opened up about her kidnapping several years ago and the nightmares that followed. This message was the most troubling she had received.

Dearest Katherine,

I promised you would be the first to know when I came to the end of my journey. I have arrived, except for one "loose end," but more on that later.

As you know, for most of the past nine months, memories and dreams have dominated my world. Until recently, the present had little influence because I could have memories in the middle of anything and my dreams had no competition.

Let me start with dreams because they have been important to both of us and they give me the greatest hope for my remaining task.

Normal adults have no order from one dream to the next. There is order within dreams but not between them. As a regressed adult, according to Dr. Ali a unique one, I had vivid replays of past dreams, beginning with childhood and ending with adulthood. I dreamt as a child, as a teenager, and as a young adult, all within the past nine months. The upshot was I became a lucid dreamer, and moreover one who could use dreams to solve problems. BTW, I can still ride magical fabrications of the subconscious for entertainment and random insights.

In a sense, I have led my life twice and from that view I have found no unsolvable problems, except one. Even for that, I don't despair because what happened is always in my thoughts. which means it will be exposed someday. You might say, I'm giving my subconscious a hard time by forcing it to look at "crime scene" photos as much as my conscious mind can stomach.

Katherine, forgive me for not telling you if I do find him. I can't bear this pain much longer. I remember Caleb so well, magnified twice, three times if you count the hours and hours I spent looking at videos of him alone, with me, and with other people. I feel like screaming, "My dear Caleb, why didn't we make a sex movie? Every position we ever tried; and the kissing before and after; and the showers together." I have lived nine months without him. I grew up watching him. He fucking well should be here!

You and Joe can look back on yourselves as children, teenagers, and young adults. That is all you can do. I could look forward as well. Nothing was in the future of course, but when I began my regression at five almost everything looked like the future, and a future with confusing contexts. The contexts became clearer as I continued studying the photos and videos, with relieving bouts of exercise and music. I got every photo and video from home and all those relatives, friends, and my lawyer could find. There were hundreds and still not enough. In-between I ran, punched, and kicked every day and played piano sometimes all night.

To put it simply, the unrelenting review of my life forced my childhood to recede. So once again I can only look backwards. Achieving that goal has been a mixed blessing. Although the friendships, successes, and loves are sweeter, the humiliations, failures, and losses hurt more. I can't say which will win. There is only one way for me to find out and that is to come back to New Haven. I intend coming back next month to begin preparing for the Eighth Annual Thanksgiving Charity.

Please don't be angry, Katherine. Your friendship is precious to me. One day a friend will give a friend a present and no one will object.

Adaline

Gutierrez and Bellingham drove to Massachusetts two days later.

* * *

Adaline, Mrs. Durand, and the detectives were sitting in Mrs. Durand's living room. After Gutierrez questioned Adaline about the attack, she tried convincing her not to move back to New Haven.

"The County Police have your descriptions and have blood and even a tooth from one of the attackers. DNA from the blood may match a name in the Combined DNA Index System, and that man will lead us to the man or woman who hired him. Even if he refuses to give us a name, we can search his phone, car, and more. Adaline, we can catch Caleb's killer."

"If you get a match, if you find my attacker, if he names the killer..."

"We have a person of interest from other evidence. If the assailant's testimony points to the same person, we've got him." Gutierrez cringed at her mistake.

"Him? Who?"

"We only give out names after an arrest. Please don't go. We *can* catch him. Joe and I are good at this."

"He is one of last year's guests, right? I have the list and can do research as well. I think you also underestimate me about security."

Although not happy about it, Katherine was impressed by Adaline's confidence and determination. She was not the same person family and friends had described during interviews when Adaline was in the hospital. Katherine didn't ask why because she knew Adaline would expect her to understand. Bellingham wanted it spelled out.

"The Charity will honor Caleb and give me back part of the life I was living. What is the alternative? Wait for you to catch him? Frankly that sounds more probable to you than to me. Or should I live behind walls until I'm seventy and *still* be afraid? Do you see any signs of him giving up?"

During the drive back to New Haven, the detectives discussed the meeting. Bellingham said, "She reminds me of you, which means she has a better chance of finding and killing this guy than being killed." They were husband and wife as well as partners.

"Not enough to make me relax. We must catch this bastard. Life in prison instead of a bullet is still justice for murder."

* * *

Adaline sent out invitations to the same patrons as last year. Because it was the anniversary of her husband's murder, a murder yet to be solved, they would be shocked and disapproving but their delight in the eccentricities and their morbid curiosity would bring them.

Adaline's appearance at the front door was stunning and mystifying. Because she had been shot in the head a year ago and attacked again several months ago, no one expected to see an extraordinarily fit, vibrant host. Her bare skin had a lightly tanned, healthy complexion and her body was slender and distinctly muscular in the sleeveless, tight-fitting gown. The gown was a dark purple with a deep neckline that accented the ruby necklace hanging in the cleavage of her breasts. There had been no news about the necklace being found.

Adaline made few mistakes with the guests' names, but even believing she had amnesia most were puzzled by her formal manner. As the guests moved towards the banquet room, many commented on the presence of the nightingale floor. It wouldn't be the first time they would declare something in bad taste. Good taste would have been removing the object so intimately associated with her husband's death. The guests had accepted the claim fabricated last year by journalists that the presence of the floor proved the Claydens lived in fear for a specific, unknown reason.

At the beginning of previous parties, Caleb would chat with guests while Adaline played classical music on the small stage in the banquet room. That night she ignored everyone as she made her way to the piano. During her recovery, her music tastes changed, with sensual jazz and old blues replacing her classical repertoire.

She began with the blues classic *When You Got a Good Friend*,[5] with singing, which she hadn't done to more than a few people before. Even when she followed it with *We're All Alone*,[6] most accepted she was paying tribute to Caleb, though in an odd, tasteless, way.

When she played and sang the sexy *Peel Me a Grape*,[7] many began to believe she was singing about a new lover, which if true was horrendously vulgar. Several old couples left.

She stopped and walked to the front of the stage. Those still standing made their way to tables. Adaline began. "Welcome to the eighth annual Thanksgiving Charity Party. As every year, I thank you for your generous support for the worthy causes listed on the front of the menu. Please permit me to say a few words about my reasons for continuing this charity. It was of course a great joy to Caleb to bestow some of our good fortune and *yours* on worthy institutions, such as our beloved Yale.

---

[5] Robert Johnson.

[6] Boz Scaggs.

[7] Diana Krall.

"We also both enjoyed presenting our novelties each year. As you all know and have been great sports about, they began as gimmicks to pull you away from your important tasks and to lighten the pain of opening your checkbooks, or however you send your millions hither and dither."

Those giggled who thought her joking, and those frowned who thought her naïve.

"Over the past three years, we have had the nightingale floor, the Da Vinci staircase, and the uncaged, illegally exhibited, tiger." She looked around the room with a broad smile. "You must remember Caleb yelling, 'It's only an old pussycat,' which of course it wasn't."

"Scared the crap out of everyone," one of the younger guests shouted. "It was glorious."

"Yes, it was," Adaline answered. "This year's treats are admittedly self-indulgent. I will explain. As you know, the wound I received last year caused some psychological distress. It wasn't, as reported, amnesia."

"Why are you acting like you don't know us?" one of the older patrons asked. He sounded more curious than annoyed.

"That is the perfect question, Dr. Faraday. Because I don't, *but* I believe I will. My memories haven't been erased or even hidden. They were jumbled up, with those from my childhood stronger than those of recent years. Most of the jumble has been cleared away, and I'm hoping this event and specifically seeing all of you will help me clear away the last hidden memories. Please do not feel used. I would have put on the charity even with no hope of that happening. I do remember Caleb more than you can possibly imagine and wish to honor him."

No one understood what "more than you can possibly imagine" meant, and some began to doubt her sanity. One of the men and women smitten by her looks and behavior shouted, "I'll drink to the lovely Adaline getting all her memories back."

"Yes, let's drink and eat. As in the past, the waiters will get you anything you wish to drink, The dinner for the first time is self-serve because I want you to try at least a few new foods. We have forty-three different dishes from around the world. One dish for each of Caleb's years."

She paused and stared at the crowd. She looked at everyone. They thought she was trying to evoke memories, but she was taking a memory shot. As she scanned, those who stood out in some way, by staring right back or shying away, got longer looks. She finished and said, "While you eat, you can listen to the quartet here or listen to me with the blues band in the covered, heated patio. I will talk to you again."

Several more couples left, too rich to get in any line. Those who remained wanted to learn whether Adaline would recover hidden memories that night and specifically if their face and conversation had been important. Their problem was she wouldn't look or talk to anyone for longer than a few seconds. She now had memory-to-face for many guests, and found few of them pleasant. It puzzled her why she had once been so respectful. After tonight, she would have parties with academics, martial artists, musicians, artists, dancers, and writers. Some of the geniuses with money also had other skills and loved the arts but were few. One day she would sort through this lot and have those with non-monetary souls join the others.

For three hours, Adaline played with the band, some classic pop and a lot of classic blues. When she finished, less than half the audience had remained. Adaline sent the musicians and employees of the catering service home. She went back to the banquet stage.

Earlier Adaline had conceived of a game she could play with the guests. It would be an Agatha Christie kind of game with everyone voting for who was most likely to be a killer. When the people began to leave in disgust, she would say, "Wait! Don't you want to know how many of your friends and neighbors believe you capable of murder. It seems to me if there was even one, you might want to change. OK, I will only mention who got the most votes. No?" She would yell, "*Then I will tell you who got my vote!*" It would have been melodramatic but foolish and costly without proof. She had a name from a dream, but who could trust dreams?

"My friends. Thank you again for coming for the charity and for myself. Yes, your presence has open memories from the last charity party and before." She bowed. "I thank you and Caleb thanks you."

Everyone believed the mention of Caleb meant she knew the name of the killer. Gasps and exclamations escaped every mouth. In her last act of vulgarity, she looked at her phone briefly and said, "Good night. Mrs. Ferrante will see you out."

* * *

After the last guests and Mrs. Ferrante left, Adaline opened the library door and walked towards the bookshelf hiding the safe. She had a phone in one hand, but no necklace around her neck. John didn't shoot because he had to know where the necklace was. She turned towards the disguised door and opened it. Without facing John, she said, "The necklace I wore tonight wasn't the original. Do you have any idea how rare a purple-tinged ruby of that size is? How magnificent? But not to worry, if it ever appears in public again or passes through the hands of a reputable jeweler, I'll get it back. It was scanned microscopically, and the photographs widely circulated."

"Adaline, I have a gun. Turn around."

"Why, John? You shot me from behind before." She turned and raised her hand with the phone. "Nightingale floors, John, electronic nightingale floors everywhere streaming into my phone. Of course you have a gun, which by the way is full of powderless bullets."

He pulled the trigger. When the firing pin hit the shell case, the primer made a surprisingly loud pop and pushed the bullet into the barrel where it stuck. He didn't understand what had happened until he ejected the empty shell. Even live cartridges were no good now.

When he looked up, ready to leap at Adaline, he saw Detective Gutierrez standing next to her. He assumed the detective was there to arrest him until he saw her handing Caleb's Colt to Adaline. She placed several boxes on a nearby desk. Adaline would replace the doctored cartridges in John's gun after removing the jammed bullet. She would wear cotton gloves and force John's fingerprints onto the cartridges before inserting them into the magazine.

To John, Katherine said, "I brought several calibers but guessed you would have another 9 mm." She turned, kissed Adaline on the cheek, and said, "Goodbye, my dear." The gift Adaline had given Katherine was herself and all the luxury with her.

After Adaline had returned to New Haven, Katherine visited her often. They became lovers after Katherine told Adaline about Emily, a beautiful young woman Joe and she had saved from being framed for the murder of her twin sister. Emily was suicidal afterwards, as Katherine had been after her kidnapping. They lived together until Emily left to be with her sister's former male lover. Katherine loved Adaline for much the same reasons. She had also come to believe Joe and she had no prosecutable case against John, the most likely perpetrator. Joe would suspect her involvement but would keep it to himself. As her husband, he had accepted his wife's bisexuality; as her partner, he stood and fell with her.

"You're the cop investigating..."

"Caleb Clayden's murder and repeated attempts to kill my lover. I was never here. Too rich for this poor Hispanic girl."

"No, Katherine, not for you." It remained to be seen whether it would be for Joe.

When the two women kissed mouth to mouth, John lunged at Adaline. It was a mistake believing she would hesitate as Caleb had. Katherine had trained her to handle the Colt proficiently and she had the mind set to shoot. She shot him in the right thigh. The two women stepped back as he fell to the carpeted floor.

"*Really* not here," Katherine said. "I *will* be with Joe soon after you call 911. Give me as much time as you can. Time of death is never certain but don't wait long." They kissed again, and Katherine left.

The large caliber bullet had shattered the femur as it passed through the leg. He lost a lot of blood before slowing the bleeding with one hand on the entry wound and one hand on the exit wound. The pain was excruciating but he had to keep her talking. "How?"

"Since we have time, I'll explain." She sat in a straight-backed chair judiciously far from the desperate man.

"It wasn't as simple as remembering Caleb calling your name. Not by a long way. Among all the fucked up things the bullet did there were several good things—don't think for a moment I'll thank you. One was learning to solve problems using dreams. In a strange twist of my mind, that ability was very unlike my memory experience. I've got what you could call 'unique in the known history of man' memories but also the well-known ability to control dreams and use them.

"I first made a video of me traveling my front door to the back gate, going through the house and over the balcony rail, and I studied videos of previous charity parties. They formed the stage for my lucid dreams. The subconscious only had to supply the main actor. It's a database of hidden memories after all. The stage was of course soaked in the context of Caleb's murder, and my subconscious eventually vomited you up. Would you like to hear about the telling dream? Sure you would.

"With the stage prepared, I traced your supposed trail while thinking of murder, though not of Caleb of course. Rather I thought of someone who had been at the party, capable of murdering a friend, desperate for money, and possibly drugged. Night after night until you finally appeared, were vomited, as I said."

She was almost finished. “One last subject. My necklace, and by *my* I mean it was made for me. What did you get for it?” When he didn’t answer, she raised the gun.

“Four hundred thousand.”

“So Caleb’s life was worth two hundred thousand dollars and mine the same. What cheap, nasty hole on earth did you crawl out of?”

The only thought he could hold onto was her killing him. He pleaded, “Adaline, we were lovers. I wanted to love you not hurt you.”

“We were sex partners once to my great shame. Caleb was my lover and now Katherine is. Among other things, your bullet has expanded my sexuality. I will fuck Katherine on the nightingale floor, but it will be my second nightingale song. The first will be me making love to Caleb’s memory. Perhaps Joe will add a third song.

“Goodbye, John.”

From Tulips to Emeralds

"I wanna, I wanna, back, back, back, back it up, back, back, back, back it up, and do it again…."[8] the two cyclists sang but not in unison.

"Too many *'backs,'*" Else shouted.

"Back, back, back, back…" John added more.

The anticipated sex was heightened by dope and beer, and the energy had to go somewhere. The coffee shop that afternoon may or may not have sold coffee, but it did sell "amnesia;" and in their favorite bar that evening John and Else drank stoned. For the location, there had been no choice because only *t'oude Pothuys* had music every night throughout the summer. The music was played by amateurs covering American and British tunes sometimes quite well but always it seemed with oddly flavored resolutions. Some nights had tall, fit, smart women from the exquisite concentration in Utrecht. Else was one of the thousands of university students who filled the city with young sex.

The lovers wandered over the bike lanes and occasionally into the roads without concern. This was Utrecht where car traffic was negligible at night, and this was The Netherlands where cyclists were never at fault. Perhaps the weed had been well named because John led Else down Kaanalstraat. Since the second confrontation with a group of teenagers, he had begun entering Balistraat from Vleutenseweg. The boys were Muslims, which meant they were potential terrorists, or so John believed because he believed Islamic leaders could reach out to any Muslim. That in turn meant they were predisposed to violence.

He hated being a coward. He was bigger and stronger. He came from an old New England family. He was a Ph.D. student at one of the world's premier universities. He was wealthy. What were they in comparison?

Kaanalstraat began at a T-intersection marking the eastern border of the Lombok District. On the right was the Ulu Moskee, which by Dutch liberality housed two large restaurants on the ground floor. On the left and for the next half dozen blocks were fruit and vegetable markets, bakeries, groceries, hair salons, and restaurants, all small and run by Turks or Moroccans. Non-Muslims shopped comfortably there.

Past the mosque, John realized his mistake and told Else to be quiet. From there to Balistraat was four short blocks.

As they did almost every day until three or four in the morning, the boys smoked hashish near the intersection with Balistraat or the intersection with the next side street, Riouwstraat. Their religious sacrilege loosened their tongues increasingly through the night, with shouts becoming more frequent, all within a dozen or so meters of John's bedroom window. Except when it was unbearably hot, he closed the window. Dutch frugality wouldn't permit air conditioning even in apartments advertised as luxuries.

---

[8] Caro Emerald *Back It Up.*

Three boys were sitting on a protruding edge of a window of the Happy Shop, the local dispensary of drug and sex paraphernalia. Two were standing facing John and Else as they turned into Balistraat. The larger of the two shouted at John in Turkish or Moroccan Arabic. John didn't understand the words but understood the ugly, angry tone.

"*Fuck you!*" John replied, followed by "*Opzouten!*" because the boys had hijacked the universal obscenity.

The entrance to his apartment building was nearby but they had to lock up their bikes. The closest bike rack had a dozen slots and some space for a few more parallel to the street. All were taken. As they walked their bikes to the next rack away from Kaanalstraat, John told Else about the boys hanging out there every night. Before they reached the rack, one of the younger boys ran up to John. He spoke in his native language and Dutch, sometimes mixed. Fear of the boys carrying knives kept John from giving the boy a shove. High or sober, all five wouldn't have worried him because he had fought big men and played football. He turned to Else and asked what the man had said in Dutch.

Else stopped moving her bike towards the rack. "You photographed them."

John laughed. "Yes, and scared the little bastards."

Else didn't translate.

Two weeks earlier, John had videoed the boys from his bedroom window to convince the landlord he needed to change apartments from the Riouwstraat side to the Balistraat side. He did change but so did the boys, ironically because of the landlord's complaint to the police. Last week, night temperatures were in the high twenties, and he chased the boys away by taking a flash photo out of his window. When the boys ran off, John laughed wildly. When no police came that night or the next day, the boys guessed they had been duped. When John tried the same trick a few days later, a screaming bout of "fuck you" scared him into making another video.

John knew the Dutch word for police but wanted something stronger. He asked Else what the word for murder was. When she didn't answer, he grabbed her arm.

"*Moord.*" She freed her arm and rode off.

He was too angry to follow. He stepped closer to the boy. "If I scream '*politie*' and '*moord*,' the police will come for you and your friends."

The Dutch words chased the group away.

* * *

It was another night of smoking and drinking, one of the last before he had to return to New Haven and resume classes at Yale. He didn't want to go. There would be no football because he had missed the pre-season and was in such poor condition he couldn't try out as a walk-on. More importantly, Else was here. That she hadn't come back to *t'oude Pothuys* since the encounter with the Muslim boys revealed how angry she was. Tomorrow he would go to her apartment, beg her forgiveness, and offer her "tulips to emeralds" again. She always chose tulips because she wanted something more meaningful from him, and tomorrow he would tell her about the resolution of one of his two problems at school.

As he finished his last beer, he thought about the second problem. "Copying her on my agreement with Gerald must have appeared mean, but..." The amnestic weed had nothing on the hash his friend Koen had given him earlier, hash that truly gave him brief bouts of amnesia.

John waved goodnight to the barman and waitress and left. The bouts continued during the ride back to Lombok. "How did I get here? Is this the right way?" He laughed at the billboard of a woman hiding her naked bottom with a "pussy in front of her pussy," but couldn't understand what she was advertising.

From habit, he took Vleutenseweg. The four lane road had a grass strip and bike lane on either side. On the south side, the bike lane was between the grass strip and a one-way car road. The road was lower than the adjacent bike lane. John rode the wrong way down the parallel road.

As he approached Balistraat, a figure in dark clothes and a black helmet dashed towards him. Because the buildings had flat facades up against sidewalks, the attacker had hidden behind a car. John saw a shadow, but then it wasn't there. It was his last amnesia. As he rode past the shadow, a knife blade passed across his throat. Blood gushed out of his neck while his legs continued to pedal. Within a few meters, his collapsing body caused the bike to veer into the curb separating the road from the raised bike path. The front wheel twisted sharply to the right and John fell forward with his left leg under the bike and right leg over it. The dark figure watched for a few seconds before running off with knife in hand.

No cars came along. Even if there had been traffic, the occupants would have missed the fallen body and bike because of the distance and the sunken road, though the area was well lit. At three in the morning, the few cyclists were all going west away from the central city on the north side of Vleutenseweg.

* * *

Senior homicide detective Inspector Frans Visser was not home when he received the call from Chief Inspector Koning. Many late nights, he wouldn't have been able to find his home. He sat up in Katrien's bed with another headache that paid for the night before. Although he had guessed from the number on the phone some *klootzak* had killed some other *klootzak*, he wasn't prepared to hear the victim was a Caucasian in Lombok.

When he arrived at the crime scene, cyclists, pedestrians, and drivers were gathering outside the cordon made by a constable and five patrol officers. To a man and woman, they were annoyed until they saw the uncovered body. By phone, Visser had ordered the constable not to touch or cover the victim. He knew that meant hearing the spectators voicing their shock and distress on *RTV Utrecht*.

"Big, fat boy," Visser said to his deputy, Sergeant de Wit. The victim's head was turned face down to the left and his lower body twisted to the right by the bike. A large fan of blood spread from in front to his left side. Visser wanted to look at the man's wallet but knew the chief of forensics would file a complaint.

Leaning against his bike was the young man who had found the body on his way to work at the Central Train Station at 04:48. The first constable at the scene had collected his statement and scanned his identity card. After hearing the man's brief account, Visser told him to wait for the crime scene team to scan his body for blood.

When a bus of twenty constables and patrol officers arrived, the inspector ordered them to chase the spectators farther back from the body and search down Balistraat and the parallel side roads for a weapon, almost certainly a long bladed knife, and discarded clothes. He told them to inspect the large rubbish bins near Kaanalstraat thoroughly, which meant opening every garbage bag.

As he resumed surveying the crime scene, the Utrecht unit of the Forensic Institute arrived. Visser approached the Chief of Forensics, Dr. de Groot. "I need his wallet, phone, and his house or apartment key." When de Groot didn't reply, Visser said, "I must make sure there are no other victims. It will be on your head if someone dies because of a delay." It was one of the pranks they played on each other.

The Chief still didn't reply. He played a prank in turn by ordering the forensic photographer to take photographs from many angles. When he retrieved the victim's wallet, both men were dismayed to learn the victim was an American, probably a tourist. They knew it meant *ouwehoeren* from the American as well as Dutch media. The victim's American driver's license identified him as John Randall Flint, twenty-six years of age, from New Haven, Connecticut.

Because there was no Dutch address in Flint's wallet, Visser needed the phone. But for a forensic scientist, phones were the goldmines of many investigations. The chance of Visser destroying evidence while searching the phone directory was very small but it was still a useful excuse to keep it out of his hands. He wrote down half a dozen Utrecht numbers. All were identified with women's names. "Good luck," he said mocking Visser's well known womanizing.

From the landlord's assistant, one of the women on the list, Visser learned Flint's address and he had been living there since the first of June. Chief de Groot removed the keys attached to the built-in bike lock, lifted the fingerprints on all four, and handed the building and apartment keys to Visser. He kept the bike and chain keys.

The Inspector found neither bodies nor signs of violence in the apartment, which was less than a hundred meters from the crime scene.

When staff from *Algemeen Dagblad* and *RTV Utrecht* arrived, he didn't try stopping the cameramen from taking photos and videos at a distance because the newspaper and TV station would be inundated with close phone camera shots by the earliest onlookers. When the reporters demanded information, Visser said he may be able to divulge the victim's name by evening. At that time, he would request people who knew the victim or had seen him last night to contact him.

All of Flint's belongings along with the body and bike were taken to the Institute's central lab in The Hague. No weapon or discarded clothes were found, but another body with its throat cut was. A Moroccan boy was buried under black garbage bags in one of the corner dumpsters that served shops on Kaanalstraat near Balistraat. The dumpsters had been searched last.

* * *

The murders in Lombok had many potential repercussions. Although the Chief of Forensics believed the American had died first, he couldn't be certain. That uncertainty admitted both the possibility the American was murdered first as an act of terrorism and the possibility the Moroccan was murdered first as an act of cultural or religious hatred.

The death of the American was of less concern to the Ministry of Security and Justice. Across the country, Muslims accounted for five percent of the population, but in Utrecht it was three times that and in Lombok many more. That a Caucasian, a Dutch national named Theo van Gogh, was murder by a Moroccan in 2004 greatly added to the government's concern. Although van Gogh was shot eight times before his throat was cut, references to the killing in media coverage of the Lombok murders concentrated on the killer being Moroccan and van Gogh's throat being cut.

Because of the horrific attacks in March in Brussels and in July in Nice, the threat of terrorism in The Netherlands was considered substantial. Security forces were on alert level 4 of 5. No government official was surprised the murders occurred in Lombok. Across the country forty percent of Moroccan immigrants between the ages of twelve and twenty-four had been arrested, fined, charged, or accused of committing a crime at least once.

* * *

Four days later, Visser met with his team of Sergeant de Wit and a dozen constables and officers. In a conference room at the Bergstraat station, he addressed the group. He had no intention of discussing the intense pressure or erroneous comments by Dutch or American officials or Muslim leaders.

He reviewed basic facts about the victims.

John Randall Flint was a twenty-six year old American from Portsmouth, New Hampshire, who had been enrolled in a graduate program at Yale University in New Haven, Connecticut. He was two meters tall and weighed one hundred and twenty-four kilograms. He had been living in Lombok since the first of June. He had no criminal record and no anti-Muslim literature on his laptop.

The Moroccan boy was identified as Farid Bensaid. He was sixteen years old and had been attending a vocational preparatory school two days a week. He was one point seven meters tall and weighed fifty-eight kilograms. His father owned the fruit and vegetable shop across from the Happy Shop, meters from where his son's body was found. Bensaid had no criminal record and no extremist Muslim literature on his phone or the family's home computer.

"At this early stage, I want to consider the most likely scenarios. First, it is highly improbable the murders are unrelated because the victims knew each other and were killed nearby on the same night by the same method.

"Those conditions also suggest both murders were carried out by the same person, which further means one did not kill the other and was then in turn killed by the first victim's friends. Neither victim had blood of the other on his hands or clothing.

"For the present, we will also not consider the killings as random selections of a Dutch psychopath, though our last serial killer was not that long ago." Everyone knew he was talking about Tristan van der Vlis, the twenty-four year old who killed seven people and wounded seventeen with a rifle in 2011.

"Before we consider that one was killed for witnessing the murder of the other, I want to review the relationship of the two men. I personally do not believe it is relevant but it was so strong and unusual that I cannot dismiss it. We have a witnessed confrontation between them and two videos made by Flint of Bensaid and his friends."

The Inspector described the testimonial statement of Miss Else Meijer. Miss Meijer had been with the victim five nights before the murder and had witnessed an argument between Flint and the Moroccan boy she later identified as Farid Bensaid. Flint had told her the boys were an unbearable nuisance every night. "During the confrontation, Flint used the Dutch word for murder, which raises the possibility Bensaid thought Flint wanted to kill him.

"The two recordings Flint did from his bedroom window of five Moroccan boys are more damning. One was done to force his landlord to permit him to move apartments. That the boys were smoking hashish we know from their conversations, and they were indeed frequently loud. The second recording is after Flint tried to chase them away with a camera flash. Bensaid threatened to kill the American. The boy had a high level of THC and a moderate level of alcohol in his blood, which may have heightened his hatred of Flint. On the other hand, the head Imam at the Ulu Moskee and his family are adamant he was not a violent boy.

"So what was it, the American being killed for witnessing the murder of the Moroccan or the Moroccan being killed for witnessing the murder of the American?" He scanned the audience.

Sergeant de Wit stood. "I favor the second. We have found no evidence of a serious conflict between Bensaid and other boys; and no one in the family has had a recent confrontation or has a long-standing feud."

"Thank you, Sergeant. There is another big reason for choosing the second option."

A constable stood. "At Flint's regular bar and restaurant, the staff reported him as eating and drinking with several different women until he met Miss Else Meijer. There was one exception. Whether he purposefully or accidentally met a man with an American accent, we could not determine. After a short bout of drinking together, they began to argue and were asked to leave."

"Yes. Good." He was confident everyone was keeping current on evidence logged in by the different teams.

"We have in total one tenuous lead. The Captain of Yale University's Police Department has already informed me he had no records of Flint being involved in conflicts on campus. When I asked the Captain to continue making inquiries, he would not make a commitment. When I asked the Ministry to put pressure on the Americans, I was told to do it myself. And so I will.

"Constable Peters, I presume your English is excellent, like all young Dutch these days. How is your crying?" He laughed.

* * *

Joseph Bellingham and Katherine Gutierrez were partners in marriage and law enforcement. They avoided letting one partnership cross over to the other except when one was going exceptionally well. Today had been a good day for police work, and they would make it a good day for their marriage.

"Let's get drunk at Archie Moore's," Bellingham suggested, though he knew their celebration would be symbolic with one or two bottles of Blue Moon and a spicy sausage pizza.

"Wait," she said when her desk phone rang. After listening for a few seconds, she turned on the recorder. Bellingham sat back down in their shared office.

When she hung up, Gutierrez said, "Joe, listen to this. I didn't get the first part but it was babbling anyway."

A young woman was crying. When Gutierrez asked her name, she didn't answer.

After becoming quiet, the woman said, "He killed him. I know he did."

"Who killed who?"

"A student," she said before crying again and disconnecting.

"It isn't hard to guess which student. She had a European accent, probably Dutch."

Bellingham said, "The Yale student murdered in The Netherlands last week. She's most likely a friend or fellow student and will be easy to find."

"The Times article said a Moroccan man was killed nearby on the same night. The two victims had a history of confrontation, which means..."

Bellingham finished her thought, "One victim was a Muslim, which further means we'll have no trouble getting help from Homeland Security if needed."

"Before we see Chief Tunbridge, let's check out Flint and his classmates. I'll call Captain Hitchens." The Captain was the senior officer in the Yale Police Department.

Within an hour, Hitchens returned her call. Gutierrez turned on the phone speaker.

The Captain informed the detectives John Randall Flint had been a student in the Department of Ecology and Evolutionary Biology and no Dutch women were enrolled in the department.

Bellingham said, "I suppose she could be a friend in another department, but I think it more likely we're being played by the Dutch police." The two detectives and the Captain could only vaguely imagine what the Utrecht police were facing with the murders of a foreigner and native Muslim.

"It is indeed possible the man in charge, Inspector Frans Visser, planted the call." The Captain had spoken with Visser and had a copy of the latest report given to the American Ambassador to The Netherlands. "So far he has only eliminated a number of potential suspects."

Gutierrez laughed. "Don't you bozos know a cry for help when you hear one?"

"Except we will almost certainly be handicapped by the Chief," Bellingham said.

The Captain wanted to do more. "We're looking for someone who hated Flint and was in The Netherlands at the time of the murder. Let me do more digging. In the meantime, you could check with Homeland Security about flights to Europe this summer by the department's staff and students. I will email you a list."

Bellingham replied, "Thanks, Donnell. I think we'll let the Inspector wonder for a little while whether his cry was heard."

* * *

When Miss Else Meijer requested a meeting with Visser, he agreed because she had been a friend of the American and because he was intrigued by the apparent mismatch between the tall, elegant Else and the fat, *bullebak* foreigner. Like Flint, she was a Ph.D. student, though in economics. It was still puzzling to Visser.

"Miss Meijer." Visser showed her a chair.

"Inspector, I have some news but first wish to know the state of the investigation. I have not heard any public announcements for several weeks."

"Miss Meijer, there has been no progress I am permitted to make public."

"In other words, none; and according to John's father the Americans are doing nothing. That is about to change. Mr. Flint has negotiated with the Yale Corporation for the Yale Police Department to provide you with as much support as you need."

"That is an unusual way of getting cooperation, but I thank you, Miss Meijer."

"There is more. Mr. Flint wants you and me to come over, at his expense and as soon as possible. He wants the possibility of an American killer investigated thoroughly."

"Miss Meijer, I confess to being frustrated with the Americans as our lack of progress here continues. I tried stimulating their interest but got no response. That problem is apparently solved, but I have another. Several Ministry officials will almost certainly denounce my leaving as an attempt to dump the case on the Americans because of my incompetence."

"Inspector Visser, do not underestimate the power of Mr. Flint's money."

"We will see. Why exactly are you here? You or Mr. Flint could have called. During our previous meeting, I saw a distraught woman but not such a committed one."

"Every media report calls John a mean, fat American. Yes, he was big and he could be arrogant and aggressive, but never with women, never with me. My guess is he committed some shameful act towards a former girlfriend. The media will never hear about that from me. One thing they do know but don't say is he was a brilliant student, as if a fat, stupid American could go to a top university. Also because he was rich, they claim money was everything to him; but they are wrong. He would have bought me anything from 'tulips to emeralds,' as he liked to say, but was happier I always chose tulips. The 'emeralds' were from our love of the singer Caro Emerald."

The Inspector was convinced she loved a man he had heard little good about.

"Unfortunately, no one else saw that side here."

"I know and want to change the public's perception and help the investigation. I have met with John's father on Skype several times, and I believe he is like his son. He has promised the Yale Corporation a substantial gift in John's name."

"What will you do there?"

"The Corporation is permitting me to disguise myself as an undergraduate student in the Department of Ecology and Evolutionary Biology."

The Inspector was puzzled. "Miss Meijer, you look more like a model than a biology student. What exactly do you intend doing as a pretend student?"

"Inspector, you are being naïve. I have shown you this model can open doors. Perhaps in New Haven, I can find leads."

The Inspector couldn't imagine what possible investigative tools aside from Mr. Flint's money she could use except sex. "Miss Meijer, that is a completely different game."

"Of course, but I am still going."

"Let me talk to Chief Inspector Koning."

* * *

The desk sergeant announced the presence of Inspector Frans Visser of the Utrecht Police Department and an associate Miss Else Meijer to Chief Terence Tunbridge. The Chief frowned. For Visser's earlier request for information, he had passed the buck to Captain Hitchens. The man's unannounced presence must mean he wanted a full investigation by city police. As a courtesy, he went out to meet Visser and his assistant but with Bellingham and Gutierrez in tow.

Visser knew from official reports, news media, and police blogs Detective Joseph Bellingham and his wife Detective Katherine Gutierrez were New Haven's elite homicide team. It was to them he had had Constable Peters send the anonymous phone call.

When the detectives heard Visser had arrived unannounced, they recognized the second of Visser's tricks. When they saw Miss Meijer, they recognized the third. The man was blatantly cunning, Gutierrez thought, coming here with an irresistible titillation and a mountain of money behind her—she knew who Miss Meijer was from the report sent by Visser to Hitchens yesterday. She guessed John Flint's father had orchestrated this or was at least paying the bills.

After introductions, Inspector Visser apologized to Chief Tunbridge and the detectives. Circumstances favored him joining Miss Meijer was his only explanation. The Chief guided everyone to a conference room. The New Haven detectives still expected a meaningful explanation from Visser. When he started to give an update, Bellingham interrupted. "Has there been a breakthrough?"

"No. That is why I am here."

Miss Meijer understood. "Chief Tunbridge, Detective Bellingham, Detective Gutierrez, I blackmailed the Inspector into coming with me. I used access to Mr. Flint's money as leverage with his supervisor. So please blame me, and I apologize." Unlike Visser, whose English was heavily accented, her English still identified her as a foreigner but produced no lag time in comprehension.

Visser explained none of his lines of inquiry had identified the one or more murderers. "I am forced to concentrate on this line because it is the one I know the least about. In Utrecht, we do not understand why we have been offered so little help when your State Department is relentless in its demand for progress. Mr. Flint has had to buy the University's help."

Gutierrez spoke. "Inspector, we understood your roundabout request and have been active."

"What do you have?" Visser glanced briefly at Else and wondered if she was relieved or disappointed. Detective Bellingham was Visser's age, though in much better condition, and Detective Gutierrez had the exotic appeal of a mature, fit Spanish woman.

"We asked the Department of Homeland Security to identify flights to and from Europe this summer by staff and students in the Department of Ecology and Evolutionary Biology. There is no way we can get the phone and credit card records of all eighty plus people. So we'll have to wait for Homeland to narrow the search."

A woman that stunning wouldn't be this man's assistant, Bellingham judged. "What is Miss Meijer's role here?"

"Miss Meijer was a close friend of John Flint in Utrecht, and Mr. William Flint has bought not only the cooperation of the Yale Police but Miss Meijer's admittance as a temporary student in the department."

Gutierrez said, "If the perpetrator is a student, Miss Meijer could become another victim. There are always opportunities on campus to catch someone alone."

"I have the University's permission." She showed no indecisiveness.

"And we do what, Miss Meijer?" Gutierrez asked.

Else gave the faintest of smiles. "Have dinner with me."

* * *

Visser hadn't been invited and ungraciously considered Else a *kut* opening her legs to an already open door. When she knocked on his door that night, he was less certain.

Else didn't enter. "I thought you would be happy to know they considered you to be blatantly cunning." She was drunk.

"Did you have a good time?" Living most nights with a prostitute was somehow less depraved than her having sex with the American detectives investigating the murder of her lover. He was drunk too.

She laughed because sarcasm from a man in a bath robe didn't have much punch. "Yes. I guessed at the meeting I would enjoy their company. You were not invited because I do not like my intelligence or sexuality being misjudged." She tapped her head against the wall twice and left. Else was John's intellectual equal, and that was the bond Visser missed.

Else had no intention of enlightening him about the dinner. The couple's openness was like John's and unlike Visser's. It was the difference between American and Dutch openness. There was more room for the bizarre in the American and dogmatic in the Dutch. By career, Visser had to be adaptive, open to the unlikely. Outside of that, he was often non-adaptive. Else hadn't enjoyed his company from Utrecht to New Haven because he said the obvious and tried to dictate the rest. More unpleasant was discovering his belief she intended using sex to "stimulate" the investigation. That discovery had been why she invited the detectives to dinner.

She was done with him. That Joe and Katherine would enjoy her company, she guessed during the meeting, from the slightly larger smiles facing her and the slightly more smiles facing away. At dinner, it opened them to what she thought and what she wanted.

They began with drinks at the bar in Else's hotel. With the first drink were deeper introductions. With the second, Else wanted to talk about the case before she got drunk. The more sympathetic they were, the more she would drink.

She began. "What would you like this pretend student to do?"

"Not something illegal. A woman as attractive as you..." Katherine said.

"Would suffer greatly in prison. I have not planned anything illegal, but self-defense is another matter."

"That sounds like you have a suspect, like a detective." The real detective giggled.

Else answer was unexpected. "The Inspector asked if John ever spoke about hostilities other than those with the Moroccan boys. I knew he loved American football, which meant he wasn't afraid of physical conflict. It seems funny now, but I was glad he was overweight because it meant he could not play that brutal game.

"It was later, I remembered John had a dispute with his research partner that remained to be resolved. I spent today with John's parents and learned more about the dispute with a colleague and also some disagreement with his supervisor. Mr. Flint said John warned him that he may need his influence at the university. He didn't know any more. I have not told Visser yet and as we Dutch say, if you throw a ball you can expect it to bounce back."

Joe and Katherine laughed. Joe said, "In other words, you are hoping it doesn't come back to bite you in the butt, as we Americans say." He had an image of himself, not some karma bullshit, lightly biting Else's naked butt. He dared not look at Katherine.

"Yes, that is more my meaning with that man," she said.

No one talked for a while. They ordered snacks to slow the effects of the alcohol.

Joe said, "To answer your question, we need the credit card information of both people, but for that we need warrants and for warrants we need a reasonable cause for each."

"If he or she was in Utrecht, the records will identify where he or she stayed," Katherine added. "Although it has been several months, the house or apartment could still have the knife and traces of John's blood." Katherine winced. "Sorry but this is important. The Netherlands

Forensic Institute should be able to recover DNA from even minute samples."

"Would it be enough if he or she threatened me?"

"Yes, but don't," Katherine said. "Remember what I said about opportunities to be caught alone on campus? A man who would murder a stranger to cover another murder is a methodical psychopath."

"Whoever killed John may have spied on him for some time and may have seen you. Don't go there," Joe said.

Else didn't want to answer. "Let's order more drinks, and dinner." The detectives' delicacy in talking about John's death and their warnings felt good, which meant more drinking. During the remaining dinner, Else avoided talking about the investigation, though not about John. She also listened.

* * *

In the morning, the New Haven detectives met with Inspector Visser, Captain Hitchens, and Else at the Yale Police Department.

The Inspector was still smarting from last night's meeting with Else. "If Captain Hitchens will arrange for me to interview staff and students of Flint's department, Miss Meijer does not need to be involved. I can always request the Ministry of the Interior and Kingdom Relations to revoke her passport if she doesn't cooperate."

Gutierrez gave a sharp reply. "Inspector, a full investigation into Flint's murder is now being conducted by the New Haven Police Department. That gives Joe and me authority over you and the investigation at Yale. The murders did not take place on a Yale campus.

"In any case, her *further* help may not be needed. Yesterday she learned from John's father that John had had disputes with both a colleague, Mr. Gerald Goffe, and his supervisor, Assistant Professor Allison Joseph. He didn't know any details. We suggest interviewing both of these people after talking to the Head of Department."

"Captain Hitchens, please arrange for the meetings," Visser said.

Bellingham said, "I hope you understand Katherine will be conducting the interviews, and your role is strictly as an observer."

The Captain nodded.

* * *

The visit to the Head of the Department of Ecology and Evolutionary Biology became largely a courtesy visit because she knew of no controversies involving Flint and staff or other students. She did say she would not be surprised because Dr. Joseph had an abrasive personality.

Visser and Gutierrez talked next to Gerald Goffe in his office. As usual, the interview was recorded. Goffe shared a grant with Flint because the two men were conducting parallel time-related research on rainforest ecology. From the academic and medical records of John and Goffe, they presumed John had been the dominant partner academically as well as physically and almost certainly behaviorally.

After introductions, Goffe said, "It was hard for me to believe because I had seen him a few days before in Utrecht. And that strange murder of a young Muslim boy on the same night. Have you linked the two? Have there been any arrests?"

Gutierrez replied, "The Dutch police believe the Moroccan boy was killed because he witnessed Flint's murder." She saw no incriminating responses until he suddenly stood and asked if either would like coffee.

"Yes," Gutierrez said. When Visser simply shook his head, Gutierrez assumed he was being sullen over his limited role.

When Goffe finished preparing her coffee, Gutierrez continued, "We're interested in your relationship with Mr. Flint. We know you both had to cooperate because of a shared grant, a quite prestigious one I believe."

"We were friends, not friends, and friends again. What exactly do you want to know?"

"Were you the American he argued with in a bar in Utrecht?"

"Yes, but outside we agreed to keep a personal review project going, though without our supervisor, Dr. Allison Joseph."

"Explain, please."

Goffe removed his phone from a pocket. After searching, he presented Gutierrez with an email from three days before the murder. It was a return email confirming co-authorship on a review of rainforest ecology. "Please note Dr. Allison Joseph was CC'd, which I was against, and John would have been the senior author, which I accepted. We intended it to be a large, scholarly review, which in hindsight seems quite naïve for two graduate students. Whether I will continue alone is uncertain."

"But why go to The Netherlands to talk about the project? Why not wait until he came back?"

"Because I felt forced to go. There had been some open animosity before summer, and Dr. Joseph threatened to have us both thrown out of the university if we didn't settle our disagreement. John laughed and left the country. It took me some time to realize the warning was about sharing authorship and if she didn't get the answer she wanted at the beginning of the semester, she would try to fulfill that threat. So I got my butt over there and we cleared the air. I finally learned why John dared stand against her. He was protected by his father, a big donor to Yale. John told me not to worry because Joseph knew her job was in his hands."

"Was Dr. Joseph so toxic as a partner? Why didn't you simply add her name to the byline if you didn't want her contributions?"

"Detective, haven't you heard the expression, 'academia is a den of vipers'? The seriousness of this business would make a gangster blush. *For example*, the fewer the names on a scientific publication in a top journal, the better for those named. Understand?"

"Yes, Mr. Goffe, it isn't that deep. It means Joseph wanted to replace you."

"That is my guess, and making him her lover again. Forgive me for saying but I can't imagine she has many admirers and John was generous with women in many ways."

"From tulips to emeralds," Gutierrez remembered Else telling Joe and her at dinner.

"Detective, I must attend an important seminar in a few minutes. Can we continue after lunch? I will make my phone, iPad, apartment, whatever, available to you then."

"One question before we meet later," Gutierrez said. "You stayed in Europe for five days after Flint's murder. Why? You must have heard about it."

"I attended the conference on climate change in Brussels for three days after the presentations because frankly I didn't want to face questioning by staff and students as John's partner. By the way, Dr. Joseph was also at the conference."

* * *

Aside from Joseph being Flint's supervisor and possibly having an academic disagreement with him, the detectives now had a third reason for interviewing her: A possible sexual relationship. At least according to Goffe, though not Else. She didn't believe it. "He rarely talked about the department or his research, but I remember him once saying no one liked his supervisor."

Visser dismissed her opinion as jealousy but Gutierrez kept an open mind. Goffe's lying would throw suspicion heavily back on him after he had laid it heavily on her.

Dr. Joseph was as advertised. The first interview ended with Joseph being taken downtown in handcuffs. Detective Gutierrez had started with a question about Joseph's relationship with Flint but soon had enough of the assistant professor's arrogant replies.

Bellingham, Visser, and Else stood outside the interrogation room. Joe nudged Else as if to say the smug academic was about to be wrenched out of her superior world.

Inside the interrogation room with Joseph, Gutierrez said, "You will answer my questions truthfully or I will keep you for forty-eight hours at the New Haven Correction Center where you'll almost certainly have unpleasant company."

When Joseph screamed for a lawyer, the detective replied, "You are logged in as arriving here when I say you are." It was a lie but until Joseph explicitly declared her intention to be silent, she was fair game. In any case, Gutierrez didn't think it would take long to get what she wanted.

"Let's begin again. I want to hear a history of your relationship with John Randall Flint. I have enough information to know if you are lying to me."

Joseph had, like Flint, retained the appetite after the athletics. Her long-standing physical aggression, self-disgust, and worry about staying on the horrendously steep track to tenure all made a civil response difficult. She dismissed the veiled threat from ignorance. "I replaced John's previous advisor two years ago. He was an outstanding student and we became lovers, but you must already know that."

"Yes, you've told me nothing. You argued over inclusion in a significant academic review Flint and Goffe were preparing, didn't you? Here is what Goffe said about the publication:

Quote, a review displaying intimate knowledge of all major aspects of rainforest ecology and proposes new ways of promoting conservation and new uses of technology would be a significant achievement, unquote. But Flint didn't want you included." She passed a copy of the agreement between Goffe and Flint to her.

"So what?"

"This is so what. To secure tenure at Yale University you need to, quote, stand in competition with the foremost leaders in their fields throughout the world, unquote; and the review would have significantly helped your weak academic position."

"Fuck you."

Gutierrez almost wished the woman wasn't handcuffed to the metal table. "Dr. Joseph, we know you flew to Brussels on the day after the agreement between Flint and Goffe was sent to you. What we don't know is whether you stayed there for the next five days. It would be in your interest to provide proof for that period."

"I invoke my right to silence and for a lawyer when you get through holding me illegally."

Gutierrez rose. "You intellectuals can be so stupid. Don't you understand your hostility gives me the justification I need to get your credit card records? It's unlikely you found a place in Europe without one."

Still outside the interrogation room, Else said to Joe, "Katherine is magnificent." To the surprise of both, Visser agreed.

* * *

After hearing from Katherine that Joseph had been arrested, Else visited her and Joe at police headquarters. "Thank you," she told the detectives and hugged both. "Last I heard, the alibis of both Goffe and Joseph were solid."

"Yes, but tell us about yourself first. You're now staying with the Flints?" Katherine asked.

"They are still heartbroken, and it has been difficult for me to leave them. They have in fact asked me to stay and transfer my PhD to Yale."

"Will you?"

"If I can make the transfer without Mr. Flint's influence, though I would have to accept his support. Graduate programs are not free at home but much less expensive than Yale."

"We both hope you stay. OK, the news. Joe has the floor."

Bellingham described the initial dead-ends. "Our Intelligence Unit found no incriminating photos, texts, or emails on any of Goffe's and Joseph's electronic devices. And forensics in Utrecht and Brussels found no evidence in any of the places either stayed. As you know, both had been attending a conference on climate change in Brussels at the time, which struck us as quite a coincidence. Anyway, dated photographs from the conference proved both had attended on the day before and day of the murders. Although Brussels is only ninety miles from Utrecht, credit card records for both in bars early in the morning of the murders appeared to rule them out."

Katherine continued. "Visser went home disappointed, as we were. They were too close physically and too involved emotionally to be innocent. Voice analyses of the interviews with both were also suspicious. Goffe was more anxious than his words suggested, and Joseph appeared to be covering her anxiety with overt belligerence.

"There was nothing to do but dig deeper, which for Joe and me meant reviewing the case over a few beers. We, I mean Joe, couldn't get over another coincidence, that of both cards being used on that morning. We realized that the credit card records only proved the cards were in Brussels at the time not that the owners were."

Joe said, "In brief, Visser was able to obtain payment records from their hotels and both bars for an examination of the signatures. One signature didn't match Joseph's others, the one of the night of the murders. Visser also discovered that Joseph had paid for parking a motorcycle at her Brussels hotel. Both facts were enough to obtain a warrant for the search of Joseph's home and office. Our forensics unit found nearly invisible spatters of Bensaid's blood on her motorcycle helmet, and we arrested her for the murder of the Moroccan boy."

"And John's murder?" Else asked.

"Visser assured us Joseph will be tried for both because of her relationship to John, the similarity of cuts to the throat, and proximity of the murders," Joe replied.

"Good," Else said.

"Yes and no, Else," Joe said. "Joseph is adamant Goffe helped her plan the murder, including the credit card ruse, where John lived in Utrecht, and his nightly habits. Joseph would not only get revenge but would also replace Flint instead of Goffe on the review.

"We believe her but unfortunately have no evidence against him. There is no ethical difference between tacitly encouraging murder and providing the means, but there is a great legal difference. If we can find a link between him and Joseph about those means, we have him.

"He played her and the stupid woman fell for it. By the way, you needn't worry about Goffe harming you. At our last interview, I made sure he understood what means we would use against him, including extra-legal if necessary, if he harmed you."

Katherine gave her husband a smile of agreement.

"So Goffe may never be caught?"

"Let's just say, he has our full attention. For example, our techs haven't finished examining all of his or Joseph's online storage accounts. Either or both may have kept incriminating emails or text messages as insurance against the other."

Katherine said, "Now, to change the subject. Tonight we would like to invite you to our traditional celebration of beer and pizza. After all we, meaning you and the Inspector as well, did catch the actual murderer."

Else brightened. "I would love to."

The Perverted Genius of Mimi Chen

It was a slow day for murder investigation in New Haven. With an average of twenty a year, it could be that way for a week or two, that is, until some miserable bastard took the life of some other miserable bastard and New Haven had more than its share of miserable bastards.

That morning, Homicide Detectives Joseph Bellingham and Katherine Gutierrez filed away their last active case. It meant they could work solely on the next murder, at least in the beginning. In the meantime they would work the cold cases they hadn't worked before. It meant dealing with poorly written reports, misplaced evidence, no follow-ups, or some combination of deficiencies that would require them to talk to the original investigator if he or she was still alive and willing. The detectives were looking for cases in which potentially incriminating evidence had come back inconclusive from the lab. They would take those to the forensic team to learn whether new or upgraded technologies could help catch the perpetrators. Otherwise, they would have to visit the crime scene (if it still existed), talk to suspects and witnesses (if alive and could be located), collect new samples (if possible), and review records of various kinds (if available).

Something caught Bellingham's eye. It was the age of a boy. "Is it possible victims of unsolved murders are younger on average than victims of solved murders? Here is a boy 12, a boy 16, a girl 6, a girl 17." All lives were supposed to be equal under the law but some deaths cried out louder for justice.

Gutierrez had her own pile of tragedies. "Look at this: A gun murder within the *Shotspotter's* range and no record." *Shotspotter* was a sound-based system that identified the location of gunshots over the covered area. "If there is a record from six years ago, we could identify where the murder took place. We know the body was moved."

"Here's your dream: *Shotspotter's* record available; apartment where the murder took place identified; killer arrested after evidence found in his apartment. Wham. Bam. Ain't gonna happen." Bellingham had the same wish but knew the probability was low. The rarity of quick resolutions was the only bad luck he joked about.

Later that day, the detectives learned the Shotspotter record had been deleted and they had nothing worth being re-examined by forensics. Bellingham unashamedly wished for a warm rather than a cold victim, preferably someone who deserved to die.

* * *

When the lights went out, Professor Merrill slapped his workbench. He had heard someone unlock the lab door and had assumed it was a graduate student, though it was well past midnight. He was angry because this was his night alone in the lab. He continued looking at the laptop until the darkness made him feel lonely. As he rose, a pistol with a silencer was jammed into his chest and fired. A small caliber bullet entered and stayed in the professor's heart.

Before the killer reached his car, a virus corrupted every document and data file in the professor's laptop.

* * *

Early the next morning, Bellingham got the murder part of his wish. Whether the victim deserved to die remained to be determined, or not.

Bellingham took the call on his side of the bed. Gutierrez rose and began to dress. It hardly mattered whether it was a case or not because they were done with sleep.

The call from Chief Tunbridge was about the murder of a Yale professor, and he told Bellingham to contact Captain Donnell Hitchens. The detectives had worked with the Yale Police Department on a previous murder, though that time the professor was the perpetrator.

Captain Hitchens informed the New Haven detectives Julian James Merrill was a forty-seven year old professor of biochemistry in the Department of Molecular Biophysics and Biochemistry. His body was found at 5:40 by graduate student Madeline Chen in the J.W. Gibbs Lab on Whitney Avenue. Merrill appeared to have been shot once in the heart. His laptop was stolen.

"So I need your help with both the murder and the theft of potentially valuable property. As you know, all research done by staff and students is owned by the Yale Corporation. As before, my techs will leave the scene to your team. They cordoned off the lab and have begun collecting video recordings for running through the body ID software. A patrol officer recorded Merrill in the lab at 11:43 last night. They will search videos from the five cameras outside the building and the two inside leading to the lab from 11:43 to 5:40. Whether the perpetrator had hidden earlier, had his or her face covered, they should have enough footage to identify something unique in his or her movements."

"They'll compare it to hundreds of hours of daytime videos of students and staff?" Bellingham asked.

"Yes. It may take weeks. Even if the killer is not staff, student, or visitor, the software and videos may eventually place a suspect at the scene."

"We'll go straight to the Gibbs lab. Have Miss Chen meet us in her office. How is her alibi?"

"I have an officer at her apartment talking to her roommate. My forensic guys did body scans for blood and powder and she was clean."

* * *

Madeline Mimi Chen entered the lobby of Xingfu Pharmaceuticals in New Rochelle. At the counter, she asked to speak to the CEO, Dr. Wu Jingyue. When she refused to state her business, the attendant refused to let her proceed.

"I will go to his home."

The attendant nervously called Dr. Wu's secretary. Chen was escorted to Wu's office by a security guard after being searched.

She stood back from his desk so he could see the full length of her curvaceous figure. She spoke in Mandarin. "Dr. Wu, my name is Mimi Chen. I am a Ph.D. student at Yale University. I am developing a nootropic drug that has shown phenomenal results on test animals. Are you interested in serving as an intermediary between me and the Chinese Embassy? Yes or no?"

"You are playing a joke, Miss Chen. How old are you?" She looked like a young teenager at first glance, but she was aging and turning provocative in front of his eyes, growing in his perception into a fit, beautiful woman. As well as age and gender, there was race to consider. "You are not fully Chinese, are you?"

His comments were irrelevant, though expected. "Intelligence doubled, tripled, and more in mice, rats, and pigs. I believe it will enhance memory to the point of being eidetic in some users. Enhanced mental energy will drive physical energy. Incredible creativity is inevitable."

"Alluring presentation, Miss Chen, and I can certainly find a job for you here." CEO's all over the world had Vice-presidents of Committees.

"Dr. Wu, if not you, someone else. Check my Yale credentials and list of publications online. After you have made a fool of yourself, I will tell you what you are going to do."

* * *

Captain Hitchens met Detectives Bellingham and Gutierrez outside the Gibbs lab. As they walked to Madeline Chen's office, the Captain said, "Miss Chen is an eighteen year old student in her third year of a Ph.D. program, which of course means she is among the brightest of our bright. Merrill was her supervisor, and she volunteered they were lovers. Her roommate confirmed Miss Chen was in the apartment until at least one."

Bellingham said, "That leaves between one and 5:40 unaccounted."

"The building and lab videos will identify when she arrived. Because Merrill had clearly been dead for some hours, we can eliminate her having killed him just before calling 911." Hitchens left them outside Chen's office.

Seeing Miss Chen for the first time was a surprise for the detectives as almost everyone. They saw an extraordinarily beautiful face that appeared predominantly Chinese but was tempered with the pallor and angled structure of a Caucasian influence. The detectives introduced themselves. Bellingham began the interview but Gutierrez would take over while he observed Miss Chen's responses and her office. He had once read elite mechanics either kept every tool in a precise location when not being used or remembered where he or she had left every tool. Miss Chen belonged to the latter school judging from the haphazard arrangement of books on the shelves and piles of papers on her desk. Despite her name and appearance, she had no Chinese decorations.

"Miss Chen, we would like you to tell us about yourself, your relationship to Professor Merrill, and what you saw this morning. Factual information. Then if you have any speculation about why the professor was killed, we would like to hear that."

Chen replied, "Mimi. Everyone calls me Mimi."

Gutierrez said, "Mimi. We know you're a Ph.D. student. Are you from mainland China?" Gutierrez had failed to see the admixture of races. Chen's dark brown almost black hair enhanced what she privately called her Chinese disguise.

"Do I sound like a foreign student?"

"So you're an American born Chinese?"

"Wrong again. I am an American hybrid. My grandfather was Chinese, and I got his dominant genes you could say. Aren't you detectives supposed to do your homework on this basic stuff? You know, like in the movies."

Bellingham said, "Cute, but a warning, Miss Chen. Lose the attitude or we will continue downtown."

The young woman gave him a smile of innocence to make his lust rise. Men didn't need to show much to be read. She guessed Bellingham and Gutierrez were lovers. With respect to his woman, she wouldn't play more with her man.

Gutierrez continued. "You are an American with a partial Chinese ancestry. I asked because of the high risk of flight by foreign students. You can be sure we'll do our homework under less urgent circumstances."

"Well said, Detective Gutierrez. I apologize." Chen gave a slight bow of her head.

"Tell us about your relationship with Merrill."

"Captain Hitchens must have told you. What more do you want to know?"

"Were you on good terms with him?"

Bellingham added, "Specifically why are you showing such a callous attitude towards the man who was your graduate supervisor and lover?"

"I told Captain Hitchens Merrill and I were sex partners. I did not say we were lovers. And as a supervisor, Julian was rapidly becoming a great academic asshole. He was the chef and we were the cooks following his recipes. Originally each recipe was big enough for a Ph.D. thesis, but recently he began acting jealous of our research. We all believed he was about to make a breakthrough that included our data."

"That was frank."

"That's what you wanted."

Gutierrez continued. "What was the research?"

"Enhanced cognition, memory, and mental energy. His students investigated different aspects of a nootropic drug."

"A brain-boosting supplement?"

"Julian would have been insulted, Detective. This supplement isn't a soup of vitamins, minerals, and amino acids. Rather it consists of engineered neurotransmitters, which are my specialty, a delivery system, an oxygen enhancer, a blood flow enhancer, and whatever he hid from the rest of us."

"The value of a successful product would be great, I presume."

"In an open market, an efficacious nootropic would be worth billions. In a restricted market, money would be less important than its incalculable effects."

"Restricted market?"

Mimi gave a look of condescension. "I will spell it out. What do you think would happen if a select group of politicians, intelligence analysts, military strategists, weapons engineers, or cultural innovators were given a drug that boosted their intelligence even by, say, ten percent temporarily. The world would gradually change in the direction they chose, with resulting shifts in political alliances, military power, culture, and more. Boost cognition higher and permanently and the world would be *wrenched* towards their desired direction."

"That is quite a leap from a drug in development to worldwide changes," Bellingham said.

"The only stake higher would be a race targeted epidemic. And believe me, *that* day is coming."

Both detectives were silenced by the inconceivable consequences of Miss Chen's predictions.

When Gutierrez recovered, she asked, "Who would most likely kill for that information?"

"Is that a serious question?"

Because Miss Chen sounded genuinely surprised, Gutierrez signaled for Bellingham not to object. "Miss Chen, we don't often investigate murders with worldwide significance. Humor us."

"The Chinese, the fucking Chinese. Who else is gobbling up technological, engineering, and medical innovations across the planet? Who else has vowed world domination since the early days of the communist revolution?"

"The Chinese revolution was a long time ago," Gutierrez said.

"Quote, for a relatively long time it will be absolutely necessary that we quietly nurse our sense of vengeance, unquote, Lieutenant General Mi Zhenyu said of the United States not long ago. I'm not going to argue history or the future with you. To get back to the murder, the department's cameras must have caught someone coming and going. I have infallible face and body recognition skills because I'm a trained *taiji* practitioner with an eidetic memory. The perpetrator will have covered his or her face, but I may recognize someone. Yes, I believe a member of staff or a student was the killer. Where did he or she get the keys?"

The detectives took a break to consider Miss Chen's extraordinary accusations and her offer.

* * *

A man in the overcoat of a major in the Chinese army sat on the bench at the southern end of the West River Memorial Park. It was cold and night was falling. He would have been unhappy being sent from Washington to meet a female student except he had heard she was beautiful and may need to be kidnapped. Major Shi was the senior military attaché at the Chinese Embassy. He hoped for the kidnapping because he had permission to beat and rape her to get information about a valuable drug. If she gave it freely, he would have no fun.

When Miss Chen appeared standing beside him, he was startled. "How dare you keep me waiting."

She sat at the far end of the bench and turned her body as much as possible towards him.

Her stare was like that of no woman he had met, including hard military women. He knew she practiced martial arts, but it was only *taiji* and she was only a girl. He knew *xingyi* and was a man; and he had backup if she ran. The subconscious thought she exuded more danger than the *taiji* and her apparent fitness warranted failed to become a conscious thought. For an elite soldier, it was an epic failure.

Without taking her eyes off of him, Chen said, "Here are my conditions. First, two perfectly forged passports, one British and one Canadian. Second, a first-in-line fee of ten million dollars within two days. Third, you will have Master Hu Shaoqi kill Professor Julian Merrill in his lab at precisely 12:25 AM on November 21st. If any of these conditions are not met, I will begin negotiations with the Russians or Japanese." Russia was the country Beijing feared the most and Japan was the country Beijing hated the most.

With her gloved left hand, she handed him an envelope containing the list of conditions, account information, passport photos, two keys, and the names and birthdates she had chosen for the passports.

After pushing the envelope deep into his left coat pocket, Major Shi pressed a button on a signaling device. His action was clumsy enough for Mimi to guess what he had done. She smiled at the Major's crudity.

"Aside from these absurd demands, what is your price?"

"Ten billion US dollars in a number of accounts." Her left hand, which was closest to him, was free. Her right hand stayed in the pocket of her bulky down coat.

When a man appeared ten meters along the track on her left, Chen turned her head to see another man coming from her right. The Major rose. "I think you had better come with me."

Chen stood abruptly and shot Major Shi in the right leg so he would collapse towards the bench. As the major fell away, she shot the soldier facing her. She crouched while pivoting and shot the soldier behind her. Both died.

Standing over Major Shi, Chen said, "The first consideration fee is now twenty million dollars. If I find you have double-crossed me in any way *again*, such as telling Hu about my demand, the final price will also double. Stop whining and call 911. I don't want to go through this with some other moron."

* * *

The New Haven detectives took a brief look at Merrill's lab and went with Captain Hitchens to the Yale Police video lab. The lab techs had found footage of the likely perpetrator both entering and leaving the building and lab.

Chen wasn't the only one with face and body recognition skills. Bellingham was what was known in police work as a "super-recognizer." He said, "Look at the way he moves." The man's face was hidden by a hood.

"So?" Gutierrez asked.

"Donnell, you are a martial artists, right?"

"Was. I see your point. He moves strongly and smoothly like one. My techs identified him as five foot seven and quite muscular. And, you'll love this, probably Chinese." The Captain knew Miss Chen believed the Chinese government was behind the murder and theft.

"How can they tell?" Gutierrez asked.

"Entering the lab, he kept his hands inside his hoodie. When he was leaving, his left hand was exposed holding the computer. A color analysis identified his skin as yellowish tan. The analysis won't hold up in court but it's evidence to follow."

Bellingham said, "I am getting suspicious of Miss Chen. She mentioned being a martial artist and now it seems the killer may also be one. Captain, do you mind if we take her up on her offer to view these videos?"

"Not at all. Her response could be interesting." And everyone liked looking at Miss Chen.

After viewing the videos, Chen said, "He isn't a student or staff, but I know this man: Master Hu Shaoqi, known in America as Sammy Hu. He teaches Wing Chun quite well and *taiji* not so well at his studio on Whalley Avenue."

"You sound certain," Captain Hitchens said.

"I am. Would you like to know if I believe Hu capable of such an act?"

"That isn't relevant Miss Chen."

"It most certainly is. It could *for example* influence how prepared you are to face him. But that's solely your problem now. On a personal note, if you mention my name to the media in connection with Hu, I will be forced to disappear. Without me, you'll never catch the person behind him." She left without explaining.

"Extreme in every way," Bellingham said.

Gutierrez was less annoyed. "She's a genius, and we know geniuses are not normal. Speaking of not normal, Alfred will be able to evaluate Miss Chen's claims." Alfred Lenz was a retired professor of biochemistry who had helped the detectives with two previous murders, one by an insane synesthete and the other by an assistant professor of psychiatry. After half a century in the US, he had the slightest of accents, with a hint of the German staccato. He continued to serve as a graduate research advisor.

While Gutierrez phoned Lenz at his home on Candlewood Lake, an hour from New Haven, Bellingham continued talking procedures with the Captain.

"Donnell, please have your tech crew covertly video Hu in case Chen isn't acting out of jealousy, spurned love, or some other vendetta."

"Certainly. Merrill had eight graduate students, three Chinese. The lone Chinese boy does not match the video because his admissions record identifies him as five ten."

"And ask your staff to arrange interviews with the relevant staff, students, assistants, and secretaries. Katherine and I will go with the CSU to Merrill's apartment later."

* * *

Three days after the meeting in the park, Chen received a registered letter with a note in *hànzi*, "Conditions accepted."

In two days, she would be twenty million dollars richer, and in five days Merrill would be eliminated.

* * *

Professor Alfred Lenz met with the New Haven detectives and the Yale Captain in a conference room on campus. Although Lenz was retired, he kept up-to-date on research conducted in the department. Like many retired academics, he couldn't let go of his love of being around other obsessed learners.

After introductions, Lenz said he understood the urgency.

"What urgency, Professor?" Captain Hitchens asked. "I need to know yours as well as ours."

"For one, the Yale Corporation will hire private investigators and demand you keep them updated on your investigation. I saw before your time here."

"Not going to happen because this investigation is also being conducted by the New Haven Police."

"Nevertheless, they will interfere and do so with the Corporation's blessing. It wants absolute control over Merrill's research and that of all of his students. There is no lack of clarity about the law here. The Corporation owns it all. Has the President asked you to confiscate the students' computers?"

"Yes, and an unpleasant task that is going to be. I have the authority to collect both university and private computers. The anger will be loud and public. We have secured Merrill's lab and office for examination by forensics and by the Chairman of the Department. The New Haven CSU has the desktop and storage devices found in his home."

Gutierrez asked Lenz about Miss Chen.

"I've been thinking about Miss Chen since your call. I attended two of her seminars, and even for an old man they were lessons in staying focused. It was difficult to look past her to the detailed information she was presenting because she is such a stunning combination of natural beauty, intellect, and knowledge. That she has publications at her age attests to her drive. And on top of her academic achievements, she is reputed to be a polymath: Piano, *taiji*, Japanese anime, and who knows what else. Blues harmonica wouldn't surprise me." He winked at Bellingham because he knew the detective played blues on a harmonica in coffee shops and bars.

"It sounds like she is quite capable of engineering the murder and theft."

"Among the staff and students I know, she would be my candidate. What I am going to say is conjecture and I hope you will keep it confidential for now. Yes, she is quite capable, so capable the murder could be far more important than the theft."

"But it's logical the murder *was* about the theft," Bellingham said.

"Imagine Miss Chen being supervised by a less intelligent, paranoiac man. Whether she had anything to do with the murder, I am willing to bet she understood Merrill's research better than he did."

"What would be her motive for killing him?" Gutierrez asked.

"The most likely is she was doing brilliant research and he wanted to claim it as his own."

"We know it couldn't be revenge for sexual assault, unless she assaulted him and he was going to complain—Joe, don't say a word. Alfred, could she have already perfected a formulation?"

"Possibly. She is that smart."

The Captain asked, "What about the drug?"

Professor Lenz was enjoying himself. He was mesmerized and didn't care. He believed Chen could bewitch old smart men faster than any other group of people. Such men had the longest history with smart women and had the best measure of her. They had all known women almost as intelligent, almost as beautiful, almost as accomplished, almost as polymathic. That was no slander on other women because none of what he understood of Miss Mimi Chen necessarily meant goodness.

"I know little but I can make an educated guess about several properties. First, the compound is so complex it can't be deformulated with present technology. Knowing the formulation is the *only* way of identifying the composition."

"A question, Alfred. Would Merrill's laptop have contained *his* formulation?" Gutierrez asked.

"Probably, though Merrill must have used encrypted files. So there is a chance the killer got nothing. Another guessed fact: The withdrawal symptoms would be brutal if not suicidal."

"How can you know for a drug that hasn't been tested on humans?" Bellingham was getting weary of grim, profound predictions.

"Imagine you are taking a drug that raises your intelligence, mental energy, and creativity, and improves your memory. Now imagine returning to what you were before. From genius to something much less is going to be unbearable."

"What about physical side effects?" Gutierrez asked.

"The most common nootrophic among students is *piracetam*, which is not approved for use in the States. It has mild and transient physical side effects. That doesn't insure a new drug won't have severe physical costs; and my guess is rapidly acquired superintelligence will lead to megalomania in many users."

"Is there any good news in all of this?" Bellingham asked.

"Assuming she did have Merrill murdered and she did develop an efficacious nootropic drug, we shouldn't conclude she will sell the formulation to the highest bidder, certainly not the

Chinese."

"Why not the Chinese?" Bellingham asked.

"Miss Chen is well-known for her academic generosity with three well-known exceptions, Merrill's Chinese graduate students. No one knows why.

"Despite Miss Chen's surname and appearance, she is an American, and may simply choose to accept the fame associated with the drug's development. It would open any door she wished to enter, depending of course on how it is used."

"*That* is beginning to worry me," Gutierrez said. She suggested a break.

Lenz rose. "I should be ashamed for speculating so wildly, though in my defense, the stakes are horrendously high."

The Captain and detectives looked mentally exhausted. Lenz laughed. "I had better treat you all to an excellent lunch." From many years of treating himself well, the professor knew the best restaurants in New Haven and for miles around.

* * *

When Major Shi opened the door to the hotel suite, Mimi Chen smiled. "Major, I compliment you on your monumental feat. Your leg must have hurt like the fires of hell while dragging those bodies to the Embassy van. You can leave." The Major limped out of the room because he had seen her right hand in her right coat pocket before.

When she entered, the Ambassador rose. With her drawn pistol, she signaled for him to sit back down. She searched the apartment for hidden guests, though she believed the Ambassador would wait to make sure the drug worked before trying to kidnap her again. He would assume she was there for the money and he could get the formulation without paying. He was wrong on both accounts.

She returned to the living room. She sat in a chair across from the Ambassador.

"Can a pig be self-conscious? Yes or no?"

The Ambassador was a short thin man. The way he had risen; his face frozen in self-congratulation; his pathetic effort to stand taller; and more told Chen much about him. She despised him before he had said a word.

"Answer the question. Can a pig be self-conscious? Yes or no?"

"I don't know these things."

"Merrill and I had joked about it being cruel to make our pig subjects smart enough to be self-aware. The answer Ambassador is 'Yes, they can be like men, another kind of self-conscious pig. Haven't you read *Animal Farm*?"

Ambassador Jiang was livid, but remained silent.

"The point Ambassador is this: Show me disrespect and you will regret it far more than Shi does."

To the Ambassador, her threat sounded hollow, but he would play along. The overwhelming delusion of being the hero who made Chinese domination of the world a reality suppressed his overt misogyny.

She put the pistol on the side table. She opened her purse and removed a bottle. From the bottle, she removed one capsule and flipped it to the Ambassador. "Take this now and leave. If I catch you keeping any for analysis, I will stop the treatment. I need to know exactly how much drug you have taken for your weight, which I'm guessing is fifty-four kilograms. In any case, reverse engineering this drug will be impossible, which also means letting that PLA doctor sample your blood every day is a waste of blood."

Ambassador Jiang couldn't imagine how Chen knew so much about what she shouldn't know. After choking down the dry capsule, the Ambassador rose to leave.

Chen said, "Two things: Come here after lunch every day for the next nine days, and you can send my order of three boys to the bar in two hours. I'm curious what the PLA's elite are like." They would be more dangerous than local Embassy soldiers, but she had ways, drugs and weapons, of making them less so, one at a time.

* * *

Before Bellingham and Gutierrez could arrest Master Hu Shaoqi, he committed suicide by cutting his own throat. Major Shi had met him in Hu's dojo and discovered all the document and data files on Merrill's computer were corrupt. The accompanying Embassy technician doubted anything could be recovered. Hu had failed to provide the Chinese government with an alternative to working with Chen—the officials had assumed Chen was trying to sell Merrill's discovery not her own. The major informed Hu he could be called on again.

Chen had warned the detectives Hu would never tell where the keys came from or who had ordered him to murder Merrill. "A high ranking official in the Chinese Embassy would have told him to obey or they would kill his relatives in China. It was how Emperors had insured loyalty; it was how Mao had insured loyalty."

* * *

Ambassador Jiang was treated long enough for Chen to judge whether there were any immediate adverse effects. She got seven days of data before the Ambassador began believing he was her equal. She had guessed the soldiers were monitoring her location day and night with hall cameras; and in the early hours of day eight, she went straight to their room on the same floor. At gunpoint, she forced all three to take rohypnol. She favored that drug because it took effect within half an hour, its effects lasted four to six hours, and users frequently experienced amnesia for the period of sedation. It also amused her giving her involuntary sex partners a date-rape drug. She left the hotel unhindered.

The Ambassador would disappear after his withdrawal madness became known to the Central Military Commission, the major Chinese branch of government searching for mental and physical enhancement methods.

* * *

"Swiss Air Flight 17 to Zurich is now boarding at gate..."

* * *

Epilogue

Mimi Chen had indeed developed a nootropic drug, and she had done it while conducting her Ph.D. research on neurotransmitter mimetics. The thesis, not Julian's work, was the foundation. She told no one and had decided the first uses of the drug would be for her revenge and her future.

First Merrill had to go. He had threatened her, not physically because he wouldn't dare. He had learned she was using equipment and chemicals not normally related to her topic. He learned because he was paranoiac. If she didn't turn over all her notes and data, he would notify the Chairman. She would be thrown out of Yale and no other university would admit her because of the impending lawsuit. His death had the added benefit of her being able to hide her formulation among the animal tests more easily than before.

Hu was her choice as assassin because he had tried to rape her in the dojo. She was attracted to him until she saw how blind he was to her willingness. He wanted violence with his sex. He was stronger but slower. The second she sensed what he intended, she went straight at him fast. While her left forearm blocked a punch, her right flattened hand jabbed him in the throat with strength. The strike stopped him long enough for her to escape. Hu was never far from her thoughts.

She knew Julian would be in the lab at least until three or four. She set the specific time because she wanted the computer virus to begin after his death. She enjoyed the irony of attaching the virus to a file ostensibly containing data he had demanded to see. The Chinese got nothing, and Hu's fate was suicide.

Major Shi had suffered enough.

After considering how she would have been treated as a prisoner, she decided Ambassador Jiang needed the same punishment as Merrill and Hu. She had a foundation of loathing for Chinese officials. Her beloved grandfather had been tortured during the cultural revolution for simply being an intellectual, and his painful accounts when she was a child created and grew that hatred. From Jiang's involvement, she got twenty million dollars and passports and learned a great deal about the People's Liberation Army with her pleasure.

No one knew Mimi Chen's goal. Lenz guessed she would kill again if it was the best solution for removing an obstacle, but that was all he could guess with any confidence.

Extras

* * *

The intruder shot both parents. The long, slender bullets entered the left eye of the man and right eye of the woman. The slugs tore brain tissue as they spun end over end. There was no mess on the babies.

It is said without dreams
we would all be insane.
But how can that be?

If dreams sometimes encourage madness,
if only a small fraction are remembered,
if most make no sense,
where is the savior of sanity?

The Memories of Killers

I'm Detective Joseph Bellingham. I offer this speculative essay on the memories of killers in regard to their killings.

In brief, I have learned that killers, like other people who have witnessed horrific events, remember nothing, much, or everything of those events. I will conjecture about these types of memories, and elsewhere you can read about murderers or defenders with each of the three types. Keep in mind the term "killer" includes defenders as well as murderers.

* * *

In the 1953 film noir, *Blue Gardenia*, the fugitive asked a newspaperman whether it was possible to forget killing someone. It's called "killer amnesia," he replied. Phony claims of amnesia by criminals, killers most of all, are of course common when alibis are feeble. Despite its apparent weakness as a defense, "I don't remember" at least reduces the chance of the perpetrator contradicting himself or herself.

Killers who develop genuine amnesia are rare. They can be subdivided into those who are never tied to the death and those who are. Imagine how different their lives are. On the one hand, the man or woman kills, forgets about it, and is never tied to the act. On the other hand, the man or woman learns he or she is a suspect in a murder but has no recollection of it. The first person may have suspicions but would still be free in body if not completely in mind. The second person is not free in mind and often not free in body. Assuming the killing was justified, we could label the fate of the unsuspected amnesiac as merciful and the fate of the suspected amnesiac as cruel. Assuming it wasn't justified, we could label the first fate unjust and the second fate as just.

If the naïve and compassionate are the most traumatized by horrific acts, women and children would develop amnesia more often than men. If true, I further infer most amnestic killers act in self-defense. Regardless of age, gender, or motive, their brains refuse to make conscious what their senses must have recorded during the act. It may be a failsafe against insanity.

A far larger class of forgetful killers consists of drunks and drug addicts. They are more likely to be murderers than defenders, though their amnesia may to some degree be influenced by the horror of their act as well as by alcohol or drugs.

* * *

The vast majority of killers remember their killings. As with all memories, some details are lost, some magnified, and some distorted with time; and the extent of each varies with the perpetrator's sanity and any number of other factors, such as intelligence, abuse, drug use, and so on. Nonetheless, they know they are guilty. They include the sane and insane, attackers and defenders, and all the motives and methods since before apes became men.

In terms of memory and killing, the explanation is simple. The human species is an extremely omnivorous predator, and such animals need strong memories of the skills used for searching, attacking, defending, and escaping. The genes of animals and men with poor memories must have fared badly in the bush.

* * *

Perfect or nearly perfect memory is inherited or evoked by great emotion, severe trauma, and possibly drugs. I have no idea how close training is to creating photographic memories, but I suspect it would be extremely difficult if even possible.

An eidetic memory caused by genes makes its possessor a permanent and continuous recorder of every sensation from birth. An eidetic memory caused by emotion, injury, or drugs makes the possessor a temporary recorder from the time of the cause. Whatever the source, the eidetic killer remembers every image, sound, smell, touch, and taste during the act of killing. Afterwards those memories are like all others in the sense of appearing both beckoned and unbeckoned. He or she can call up details at will but must also suffer their occasional appearance against his or her will. Wanted or not, the memories most likely to appear are mistakes, whether they can be corrected, and the most horrifying moments, which of course can't be corrected. If you worry about leaving hair on the victim's body, you will focus on the times you were touching him or her. If you worry about someone hiding in the shadows, you will focus on the broad visual and auditory environment. Whether appalled or delighted, you will think more often of the most intense violence.

The complete sensual recall of something as momentous as the death of another person by one's own hands can be expected to affect perpetrators in wildly different ways. Among eidetic killers, both murderers and defenders, are those who are horrorstruck and those who become obsessed. Men and women in the first group don't kill again except by accident. Men and women in the second group kill again on purpose. It is easy to visualize how killing someone, even someone you hated and had planned to murder, would be repulsive for the rest of your life. It is less easy to imagine how the repeated review of a repulsive act in full sensual detail would become attractive. It is possible some killers experience repulsion first but willingly or not experience reconciliation, fascination, pride, and obsession in order afterwards.

No one explains because no one understands,
why we created our own demon lands.
On an infested corner, in the middle of the day
my first love was slain by a bullet astray.

Hostage Takers[9]

Outside of war, an angry man with a gun is the scariest thing a cop sees, that anyone sees. The weapon is potentially deadly, but the anger is of greater concern. Consider the problems of negotiating with an angry hostage taker.

- Appealing to reason is ineffective because emotion is holding the trigger and *pulling a trigger is so easy.* Movie and TV scenes in which screaming and cursing perps, cops, or victims are talked out of shooting are bullshit.
- Making an emotional appeal is likely to exacerbate the perp's excitement, which is already committed to action.
- Angry people don't respond well to threats. Punking out is not an attractive option even for someone with low self-esteem.
- Because escapes are so rare, perps must be ready to accept the worst consequence, their own death. That means identifying other consequences rarely changes the result.
- Appeals to justice are useless because only a warped sense of justice could have led to the current predicament.
- Bribery seldom resolves hostage situations because the only gift of real value is freedom.
- Trickery is dangerous because many paranoid or schizophrenic perpetrators are extremely sensitive to being played. In other words, the trick had better be brilliant.

It should go without saying but I will anyway: Referring to a perp's mental capacity, delusions, emotional instability, alcoholism, drug addiction, criminal record, or failures of any kind are likely to kill hostages and end your career.

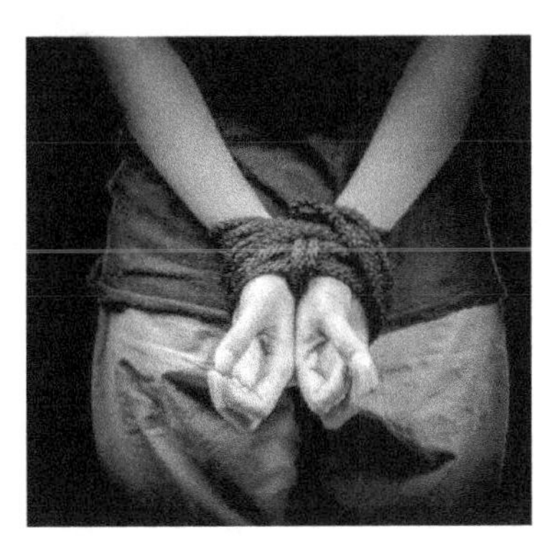

[9] Excerpt from "Armed and Angry" in *The Bellingham and Gutierrez Crime Series.* Gadfly Books. 2015.

The End